FAR BLUE MOUNTAINS

MAX McNABB

Beloved Captive Trilogy Book 1

Max McNabb is a writer from Lubbock, Texas, and the editor of TexasHillCountry.com. He grew up on the family farm near Ropesville. He's the author of the Beloved Captive Trilogy: *Far Blue Mountains*, *Deathsong*, and *Sky Burial*.

Dedicated to my parents

Scott & Amy

And grandparents

Ronnie & Sandra McNabb

Bill & Gwen West

This novel was inspired by the real events of the Fimbres Apache conflict of the 1920s, a latter-day frontier war between the last free Apaches and a Sonoran rancher. May the spirits of the dead find peace in eternity.

TABLE OF CONTENTS

Cast of Characters

Jubal McKenna: A powerful rancher in the Bavispe Valley, father of John Russell and Claudia, husband of Sara.

Dolores/Bui: Apache girl adopted by the McKenna family.

John Russell/Denali: The son of Jubal and Sara. An epileptic.

Cain: Once a legendary soldier of fortune, now a middle-aged strikebreaker who longs for one last war.

Mosby: Cain's right-hand man, a veteran of the 10th Cavalry.

Carnoviste/Apache Juan: The last chief of the unsurrendered Apaches, husband to Ishton, Tsaltey-koo, and Hanlonah. Father of the young boys Neiflint and Oblite, later the adopted father of Denali.

Gouyen: The wise woman is the twin sister of Nantan. She uses her Power of Finding Enemies to sense the presence of nearby hostile forces. Childless, Gouyen treated Bui as her granddaughter.

Nantan: The medicine man, twin brother of Gouyen. His supernatural Power ensures the band's survival and grants him authority that rivals Carnoviste's own.

Ishton: The beautiful older sister of Dolores and favorite wife of Carnoviste.

Sara McKenna: Jubal's wife, mother to John Russell and Claudia.

Claudia: Baby daughter of Jubal and Sara.

Wesley: An old ranch hand who works for Jubal.

Hector Cienfuegos: Ten years older than Jubal, Hector is the foreman of the ranch and Jubal's closest advisor.

Angel Ochoa: A young vaquero, later the fiancé of Dolores.

Zunde: Apache warrior, rival to Carnoviste for the chieftainship.

Chatto: The young son of Zunde. Also Denali's best friend.

Moroni Thayne: Mormon rancher in the Bavispe Valley.

Aubrey Eliot: Cain's old mentor, a daring cavalry officer who convinced Geronimo to surrender peacefully. He died in the Philippines during the war, but Cain is haunted by ghostly visitations.

Oblite: Son of Carnoviste, much younger than Denali.

Neiflint: Son of Carnoviste, much younger than Denali.

Matzus: The brave John Russell falsely believes is responsible for murdering his father because he showed the bloody scalp to the boy.

CHAPTER ONE

Sonora, Mexico

Spring, 1927

The girl called Owl Eyes kneeled on the rocky peak. A rawhide cord strung with dangling bells was tied about her ankle and it stretched down the sheer cliff-face and tethered her to the camp below. At her side rested a bone-handled knife and a waterbag fashioned from a deer bladder. She'd kept watch all night, alert for sign of pursuit through the broken foothills to the west, over the trail toward the river and yesterday's plundered village. Nothing moved in that darkness. Now she turned to greet the dawn with the morning prayer of her people.

She looked to the east where the sun rose fiery and misshapen above the sierras and in the breaking light she spotted them. Riders on the ridgeside. Horsemen emerging one by one from the arroyo that had concealed their approach. The prayer of thanks died in her throat.

They were coming with the sun, not out of the western dark as she'd expected, and they were advancing fast.

She gripped the long cord and pulled it taut. The small bells jangled, heralding danger. She gave it three quick pulls, then untied the knot around her ankle and cast the rope off the cliff, still ringing. It twisted as it fell, writhing like a serpent, and landed on the stones two hundred feet below. She glanced once more at the riders coming full tilt. Then she turned and ran down the switchback trail that clung to the peak's granite face.

Later she'd remember the scent of acacia blossoms.

* * *

Down in the camp they woke to the ringing bells. Women gathered sleepy-eyed infants and rolled blankets in haste. Men armed themselves and readied the packmules laden with stolen corn and household goods. The pool of water where they'd camped lay in the shadow of the peak and old folk hurried in the dimness. The children had slept with food pouches strapped to their chests against just such an event.

From the strongest warrior to the smallest child they kept an austere silence, the selfsame in victory or rout. They were the Diné, the People. Though to all others they were known by the name the Zuni had given them—

Apache, the Enemy.

The younger braves attempted to start the cattle

moving. When the chief saw them, he swung up on his horse and put the mount forward. The Mexicans called him Apache Juan, but in truth his name was Carnoviste.

In large part his title of chieftain was honorary. Among the People only those of proven wisdom and courage might claim the burden of leadership. Carnoviste's status as a respected warrior earned him his position, but he had no right to force his will on any man. They were a society of true anarchists. Any warrior who disputed a chief's order was free to go his own way whenever he chose.

Yet for a warrior to serve as chief meant he was held in high esteem. Carnoviste bore the mark of his courage, plain for all to see, a scar running from the corner of his left eye down his cheek to the jawbone. He'd taken the knife from the Mexican who'd slashed his face and driven the man's own blade through his heart. The People were proud to follow such a warrior.

Their band was the last of the unsurrendered, descended from those who'd refused to go north with Geronimo in 1886, four decades earlier. Instead they'd taken the forest passage and hidden themselves in the Sierra Madre, the mother mountains wild and free. Their lives were such that few men older than Carnoviste's twenty-nine winters were left among them.

He drew up beside the braves.

"Leave the herd," Carnoviste told them. "They won't chase us once they've got the cattle back."

"Give up the cattle without a fight?" a brave named Pericho asked. "You'll make us weak as the valley dogs."

"The People are less and less every spring, but the Mexicans always raise more cattle. It's not worth losing a brave. Better to live so you can make your woman smile and her belly fat with new life for the People."

"But if we leave the herd and they still follow us?"

"I'll fight," Carnoviste said, "till their bodies are food for the coyotes or they send me to the House of Ghosts."

Pericho stared, then nodded his assent.

Carnoviste motioned to the packmules. "Lead them out with the women and children," he told them. He would linger behind with a handful of older warriors and form a rear guard in case a running fight was unavoidable.

A boy gathered up the bell rope where it had fallen. Carnoviste looked up at the narrow game trail winding its way down the peak. His wife's young sister Bui, whose name meant Owl Eyes, had sounded the alarm. He'd posted the look-out only as routine precaution, for they held the Mexicans in contempt—and none of them had expected pursuit after their raid on Nácori Chico the previous day. Their flight from the village had been almost relaxed, bivouacking late that night at the spring and slaughtering a steer in celebration.

The villagers feared the People's wrath. They never offered resistance or gave chase. Though no one was hurt, perhaps the raid had gone too far this time, the band taking too great a plunder and upsetting a delicate balance. He still didn't believe it was the villagers who pursued them now. He reasoned that the excess of spoils the raiders had taken must have sent the villagers running to the patrón of the valley, begging help from the White Eye rancher, and so the man was coming with his vaqueros and guns.

Even now his heart wasn't fearful. They'd abandon the herd and escape where only one of their own could follow. The mountains would welcome them in.

Between the rancher and the People there was no centuries-old bloodstrife, not as there was with the Mexicans. This White Eye allowed them to cross his range unmolested, to take a steer from time to time when they needed beef. The peace had held for decades. Once the White Eye recovered the villagers' cattle, it would be so again.

Carnoviste sat his horse and waited to catch sight of the girl. No movement on the trail. The darkness slowly yielding.

Something wasn't right—Bui was nowhere to be seen. The braves led out the packmules, women and children following, and Carnoviste's wife left behind a mule for her sister to ride.

He pulled the 1903 Springfield from its sleeve and rested the rifle across the pommel of his saddle and sat the horse. He was going to wait as long as the other warriors would allow.

Across the rocky ground, Gouyen the wise woman also stood watching the trail. The line of retreat filed past her. She held the black mare's hackamore in one hand and with the other she fingered the leather bag hanging between her breasts, her talismans inside.

At her feet lay the remains of the butchered steer. Its blood had stained the rock and pooled dark and still in the rounded depression of an ancient metate. On that slab the mothers of an unchronicled nation once ground corn for their children. Callused hands wielding pestles, the granite worn smooth. Their flesh and bone long since dust on time's own oblivious millstone.

Flies buzzed over the steer. Before the day was out a pack of ragged scavengers would contend for the carcass, the victors lowering their snouts to lap bloody-chopped from the congealing pool.

Gouyen studied the trail. She scanned the shadows, hoping to glimpse Bui, intent as though the orphaned girl were her own, the daughter of her old age.

* * *

Jubal McKenna rounded the mountain from the east, leading his vaqueros on horseback. They descended the northfacing slope along the same trail the Apaches had driven the cattle. Riding with rifles drawn and ready, other men cradling shotguns. The spring lay out of sight through scrub mesquite and juniper down below.

The vaqueros spoke in low tones, eager despite a heady fear.

Jubal scratched the brown stubble on his jaw and thought about what lay ahead. He knew the vaqueros hoped for a clash against that fugitive enclave. The last dismal horde. Fabled monsters of whom their abuelitas had cautioned them, saying they loved to carry off disobedient children. The vaqueros wanted to ride down those beasts of boyhood nightmare, but for Jubal it would be enough if they could recover the cattle and best of all if it could be done without a fight.

Apache Juan's band had raided the ejido village of Nácori Chico and left the communal farmers destitute. When he'd entered the village plaza, the scar-faced brigand had turned his horse and slowly looked the campesinos over where they stood frozen in terror along the dirt street. He stared in disdain and expectancy. Like a feudal lord come down from his stronghold demanding tribute. Then in broken Spanish he called them his shepherds. He said he'd spare their lives so they might grow new crops and raise more cattle for the Apaches. The raiders took the supply of winter corn and looted the adobe hovels, seizing blankets and kitchen utensils and what baubles appealed to them and departed driving the ejido's thirty head of cattle.

When the Apaches were gone, the village sent a boy running in his rawhide huaraches. By the time he reached the McKenna ranch he was exhausted. The boy kneeled in his dirty white manta. Out of breath, he made his appeal.

Jubal and his vaqueros set out after the stock thieves, trailing them into the foothills of the Sierra Madre, sanctuary of the wild Apaches. Late in the night, Jubal had halted and looked in the distance where the trail climbed a ridge beneath a stone peak. He knew of a spring on the other side, an old Indian camp. He hoped they'd relented and taken rest there. The first light of dawn an hour to come, but the moon was almost set. They waited. After a while the moon slipped below the horizon and Jubal led them east in the darkness. He circled around to head northwest up a dry arroyo that cut down the ridgeside and they'd made their hidden ascent.

Now Jubal paused in the trail beside his segundo Hector Cienfuegos. He drew his .30-30 from the saddle-scabbard and levered a round and turned his horse. He spoke to the vaqueros in Spanish.

"We're going down there to get the cattle back—that's all. They have the corn, let them keep it. We force them to run, then we take the herd and it's over. Understood?"

"You want to let those gut-eaters screw us?" Isidro Mora said. "And get away free?"

"I'm looking for an end to this without any dead bodies," Jubal told him. "I don't want a fight and they can't afford one, as few warriors as they got left. They're not going to risk losing a young buck over some scrawny cattle. They'd just run off into the mountains

8

instead. Let them get away while they still got a place to go."

"Roll over, uh?"

Hector spoke up. "Nobody has to get hurt, young man."

"I say we kill them all, old man," Mora said. "Then Señor McKenna won't keep losing cattle in his pastures."

"If a few steers stop the blood," Jubal said, "it's a fair price. We lose more to lions than Apaches."

Mora looked over at his younger cousin Angel Ochoa, a vaquero not much more than a boy. "Can you believe this? Without even a fight."

Angel was silent, gaze downcast.

"Which is it?" Hector asked Mora. "Come with us and do like the boss tells you or go play Indian killer by yourself?"

Mora eyed the segundo.

At forty-five Hector was ten years Jubal's senior, like an older brother to him growing up on the ranch when Hector's father was foreman for Larkin McKenna. His goatee, once jet black, now sported streaks of gray and he wore a pair of glasses. Older these days, but still hard as nails. Jubal could see Mora making his appraisal, deciding correctly the segundo had no give in him.

"I guess we're coming with you," Mora said. He looked at Jubal. "What if you're wrong and they don't run? Maybe they're hungry for a fight."

"Then it's blood for blood," Jubal said.

He booted his horse forward.

* * *

Jubal rode down the steep flank of the ridge where the trail curved through dense brush above the spring. Vaqueros followed, prepared to fire. When Jubal's horse stepped out of the mesquite, the camp was empty save the scattered herd and a mule that stood cropping grass, its rope hackamore tied to a cottonwood branch.

Around the spring the slope leveled out to form a small plateau. Here prehistoric pictographs of hunters and exotic birds and pairs of bucks with their horns locked in combat marked the high rock wall. He rode past the butchered steer and past where the stone was blackened from old fires. Several cows stood drinking from the pool. One of them raised its chin dripping from the water and lowed at him.

His horse shifted and stepped, nervous at the lingering feral scent of Apaches.

"Left the herd and ran," Jubal said.

"It's good nobody had to die today," Hector said.

"Let's get them rounded up."

They put away their weapons and began hazing cattle out of the mesquite. Angel dropped the loop of his reata over the head of a spotted yearling. Hector and a vaquero named Cruz drove a group of stubborn steers into the clearing.

Jubal was moving through the overgrowth on the far side of the spring, Isidro Mora behind him, when his horse shied and bucked. A figure darted from the brush.

"Gut-eater," Mora yelled.

The buckskinned figure scrambled across the shallow pool.

Mora drew his pistol. He thumbed the hammer and fired. The bullet ricocheted off granite and the gunblast echoed in the stone amphitheatre. He fired again, but his own mount was half-crazed and the shot went wide.

The figure hopped on one foot and disappeared into a cleft in the rock wall.

"Got it," Mora said. "Nailed that little Apache." His horse was rolling its eyes, arching its neck. He put rowels to the mount and splashed through the pool.

"Hold back," Jubal shouted.

Mora reached the entrance to the grotto and raised his pistol and pulled the trigger. The shot whined off the grotto walls. He cocked the hammer back. Jubal rode up alongside and jerked Mora's arm and his fourth bullet went flying off into nothing.

"Calm down, damn it," Jubal said.

Mora ignored him and glanced back at the other vaqueros. "Let's show this Apache what we do to thieves. Who's with me?"

Hector drew up, cursing, on the other side of Mora. "Give me the pistol."

Mora grinned at him. "You go to hell."

Jubal swung. He punched Mora in the jaw, then Hector snatched the gun from his hand. Mora's hat fell off and his horse stepped on it. The vaquero sat the saddle and held his jaw.

The men crowded in front of the small cave. "Build a fire," Cruz said. "Smoke the Apache out. We'll shoot him if he tries to fight."

"It's just a girl," Angel Ochoa said.

They all turned to him. The boy looked embarrassed to have everyone staring at him. He'd only been working among them a few weeks.

"She was wearing a dress," he said. "And she's hurt, hobbling on one foot."

Jubal dismounted and handed his reins to Hector. He kneeled at the cave opening and peered into the darkness, listening.

A sound within. A groan, the faintest sigh. He got a book of matches from his pocket and struck one and lit the book entire and pitched it burning across the threshold. The flame shone in the cave. For an instant he caught a glimpse of the bright reflection in her eyes. Then she retreated deeper into shadow.

"Everybody move back," he said.

The vaqueros led their horses by the bridle reins away from the opening. They produced tobacco and rolling paper. Hector stood smoking and watching Jubal where he kneeled like a mourner before a tomb.

Jubal whispered words of good will in Spanish, too

quiet for anyone save himself and the girl to hear. He couldn't know if she understood the language, but he continued nonetheless. He didn't ask her to leave the cave. Instead he spoke to her of his life.

"My son's name is John Russell. He's eleven years-old. Maybe about your age? He's been in the saddle since he was three and there's nothing he can't do on a horse. My daughter was born last winter. We named her Claudia."

His words were soft in the stone chamber.

"You'd like my wife. Sara would make you good things to eat. I wish she was here—she'd know how to keep you from being scared."

He heard Mora ask, "What the hell does he think he's doing?" Then Hector told the man to shut his mouth.

Jubal took off his stockman's hat and ran his fingers through his hair. He kneeled turning the short brim in his hands, staring into the shadows. "What are we going to do with you?" he asked the unseen girl.

Silence the only answer.

He rose and stood facing the dark opening. "I promise I won't ever hurt you. Let me help." No longer whispering, voice full and commanding. "Come on out," he told the girl. He spoke on no authority save the truth of his heart.

Everyone watched. Jubal held out his hand palm up and charged her to step into the light. The sound of cattle drinking, the mule still cropping grass. He waited.

A face appeared out of the dark. She hesitated between the grotto and the open world, then met his eyes and moved forward and stepped blinking outside the cave.

An Apache girl about thirteen years old. Her skin the color of dusk. She smelled of earth and sweat and animals. She wore a buckskin dress with a little bag tied about her waist and beaded moccasins that came to her knees.

She clutched a crude knife with a bone-handle and went limping toward Jubal. She reached out slowly, uncertain, then took his hand and Jubal helped her to a rock by the pool. The girl sat down. Jubal kneeled beside her and held her right foot in his hands, raising it to remove the moccasin, and she let him.

Coalblack eyes watched the vaqueros. Her cheekbones high and proud, lips set in defiance—a slight trembling in her hands the only sign of fear she showed.

He was gentle tugging the moccasin free. When he saw her ankle, he was afraid it was broken, the skin swollen and bruised. She glanced down at her injury, seeing for the first time how bad it was, and raised her head and sat staring wild-eyed at the strangers surrounding her. He thought she was too frightened to register the full intensity of the pain.

"You speak Spanish?" Jubal asked.

The girl hesitated, shook her head no.

He thought this a likely falsehood, but it didn't matter. He continued in Spanish, the words unimportant,

14

speaking to her with cadence and inflection.

"I swear I won't let anyone hurt you. Don't be scared, all right? You never have to be scared with me."

He held her calf and foot and submerged her ankle in the cool water. She didn't make a sound.

Jubal looked up at Hector. "I don't know if it's broken or just a bad sprain. We need to make a poultice and get the swelling down."

"I'll go find some ocotillo," Hector told him. Curanderas, folk healers, had long used the powdered roots of the plant to reduce swelling. Hector opened his saddlebag and removed a machete in a leather sheath. He entrusted his reins to a vaquero and stepped toward the brush.

"Now can I have my gun back?" Isidro Mora asked.

Hector had placed the pistol behind his belt at the small of his back. He shook his head and walked on past Mora.

"They left the mule for her," Angel said. "Where was she that she couldn't leave with the rest of them?"

Jubal nodded toward the peak. "Somewhere up there, my guess. Standing watch."

After a while Hector returned with a handful of ocotillo roots. He kneeled and placed them in one of the ancient metates and crushed them with a rock. Jubal wet his bandana. He made a poultice of the pulverized roots and tied it about the girl's ankle. She watched without expression.

15

Jubal rose. "Get the cattle together and let's go home."

Hector stood holding the mule by the reins. "I'll fill a pack with some food, a canteen for her. All right?"

Jubal didn't answer.

"She's hurt," Hector said, "but she can ride. She won't have any trouble finding them."

"Maybe it's better she stayed down here."

"Why would she want that? The mountains, they're all she's ever known."

"All she'd ever know."

Hector frowned. The wild girl studied them.

"They'll still be up there when she's healed," Jubal said. "Hunting and thieving because it's easier than growing. She has a chance to see another way. You understand what I'm saying?"

"Do you?" Hector asked. "You know what happens when a little bird falls out of its nest? So little it can't fly yet, then a man picks it up and lays it in the nest again? The mother bird comes back, all she can smell is the man smell. She doesn't recognize the baby anymore. So she leaves and lets it starve to death."

"We're talking about people. Not animals. She could have a better life."

Hector shook his head. "You can't force salvation on someone. For her sake, don't pick her up."

* * *

16

They gathered the cattle and started them toward Nácori. Of the thirty stolen head they'd recovered all but the slaughtered steer.

Only a few vaqueros were needed to drive the small herd, most of the men riding out in advance with Jubal, Hector, and the Apache girl. She appeared to have taken a liking to Angel. Jubal had caught her casting shy glances when the boy wasn't looking and he'd invited Angel to ride ahead with them. As a new hand it should've been his duty to stay back with the cattle, but Angel was pleased to accept the patrón's offer. His cousin Mora looked on in disgust, trailing in the dust of the herd.

They took the old Apache trail out of the foothills. A dim trace used for generations, raiders coming down from the high reaches to prey on outlying ranchos and colonias, never ridden twice on the same raid. Apaches fled to their redoubts by alternate paths, suffering no chance of armed vaqueros lying in wait for their return.

Since mounting the mule, the girl had grown more confident and she'd put away her knife. She had to be in pain, but she wouldn't show it. Angel teased a smile from her by making his dun perform the Spanish walk and bow low.

They were riding through a swale of grama and goldenrod when she took from her belt a little flute made from the hollow bones of a bird. She played a simple tune. The men applauded her. She grinned and kept playing and by the time they reached the valley, there was none among them she'd failed to charm.

CHAPTER TWO

McKenna Ranch,

Bavispe Valley, Sonora

On the windmill tower the boy and the old man stood silhouetted against the setting sun. A pastureland devoid of trees surrounded them. Clusters of cattle grazing. The wheel with its fan of galvanized blades was motionless, locked to the tail. John Russell McKenna gripped the ladder and reached down where the old man stood at the midway point and took the can from him.

"Careful," Wesley said.

"I ain't goin to fall," John Russell said.

"You have one of your spells and break your damn neck, your mama'll tan my hide."

"Don't have spells no more. I'm done cured."

When he was eight years old, the boy began suffering unexplained seizures that grew in frequency and ferocity. His parents, Jubal and Sara, took him north across the border to consult doctors in Arizona. They diagnosed epilepsy, prepared him for a lifetime of the condition, then just as the intensity of the attacks seemed building toward a crippling grand mal, they ceased all occurrence. John Russell believed it was over for good, three years since his last seizure.

"Just be careful up there," Wesley told him.

The redhaired boy climbed back onto the platform. He'd already drained the old oil into a bucket and replaced the broken gear. Now he kneeled pouring the fresh can into the gearcase. Dull rose light shone on the blades and the boy's face. The McKenna brand was painted bright red across the tail of the windmill.

A big sorrel named Cricket stood waiting down below, his reins tied about a tower leg, and he flicked his short ears at a blowfly and cropped grass. A pair of mules were hitched to a buckboard beside the earthen tank, cedar posts and a roll of barbed wire in back of the wagon.

Wesley stared up at the boy and rubbed the old rope burns around his neck. A nervous habit. John Russell asked him once about the burns. A permanent reminder of his misspent youth in Texas, he'd told him, and one reason he'd never cross that border again.

"You know how come this well got dug here?" Wesley asked.

"I bet you're fixin to tell me." John Russell kicked the broken gear off the platform. It landed in the muddy

depression of the stock tank. Puddles were s
hoof and paw prints around them, but the po
since the windmill broke down.

"Your daddy cut a forked limb from a pe   ,
Wesley said. "We rode out to this pasture and he climbed
down and started walkin, holdin that limb out in front.
When he come to this spot, the branch bent so hard it
broke in his hand. He looked at me and said, Sweet
water, right here."

The windmill stood in one of the ranch's few pastures
not watered by a spring or laguna or the Bavispe River
itself. Jubal and several unlucky vaqueros had hand-dug
the well. Then a mule team and fresno scraped out the
stock tank.

"I seen him witch before," John Russell said. "He
tried to pass it on to me, but it didn't take."

"Only one in a family can do it and not ever family
has the one. I asked your daddy did he have to use a
green branch? No sir. Said he could witch with a piece
of wire. It's the man, not the rod."

The boy pulled a bandana from his backpocket and
wiped his hands and looked out across the pasture dotted
with cattle. Long grass waved in the fading light. Distant
reefs of red clouds over dark foothills.

"You figure he caught up with them Apaches?" John
Russell asked.

"Reckon this mornin sometime. Or else they give
up the chase, if the Apaches made it too high into the

mountains. Either way, he'll be back this evenin.''

John Russell knew his mother worried about the pursuit, but the boy wasn't anxious. It was unthinkable anything could happen to his father—no one matched his determination.

"I wonder what they look like," John Russell said.

"You seen Indins before."

"Not wild ones. You ever see a bronco Apache?"

Wesley spat a stream of tobacco. "I seen what they leave behind when they're in a killin mood. Hand me down them wrenches, we got to head back."

John Russell passed him the tools. He tossed the empty oil can down into the wagon. "Who'd you see that got killed?"

Wesley stared at the ground. "I come across a fire south of Fronteras. This was twenty-five, thirty years ago, back when the Apache Kid and Massai was still on the loose. It was a wagon turned over and burnin. There was a old woman layin with her skull stove in. Right next to her a pregnant girl. They'd slit her open and jerked the baby out." He shook his head. "I hadn't ought to tell you things like that. It ain't good for you to hear."

"I can stand to hear anything you got to say. Go ahead and tell the rest."

"It's just pure meanness. Start the wheel."

John Russell released the lever. The tail went sliding out, drawing the wheel into the west wind. Gears groaned. The wheel started turning and the sucker-rod clanked, stroking up and down the pipe, working water out of the darkness.

"Go on and tell it," John Russell said. "I want to know."

Wesley glanced up at him. "They'd tied the man naked to a wagon wheel and built a fire underneath. Roasted his brains out. But the worst of it was that little fella. I reckon he come out alive, bawlin, when they cut his momma open, and to shut him up or just for the sheer hell of it, they'd swung him by the heels and bashed his head against a rock."

"Damn," the boy said. He waited for Wesley to scold him for cussing, the way he usually did, to tell him he was picking up an old man's bad habits.

Wesley only said, "I wisht I'd never seen it."

Water came gushing from the flow pipe cool and sweet, spilling into the tank. John Russell pitched the oil from the rubber bucket. It splashed on a bare patch of ground away from the tower and he carried the empty bucket and followed the old man down.

Wesley took careful steps to the buckboard. His eyesight was failing and he no longer rode with the other vaqueros as he had for so many years. These days he mended fences and drove a wagon for Jubal McKenna.

John Russell patted Cricket's chest and untied the reins. "I heard it told that Geronimo started killin out of revenge," he said. He swung up into the saddle.

"Mexican soldiers massacred his family, so he went on the war path."

"I don't doubt it one bit. But that girl never massacred no Apaches. That little fella sure didn't."

"Well, who started it all then?"

"Nobody. Everbody. The devil with the damn apple. Let's go home and rest. Don't forget, tomorrow you got to help me finish that stretch of fence."

John Russell groaned.

"What's a matter?" Wesley asked. "Post-hole diggers don't fit your hands?"

"Nothin but a rope and reins. If it can't be done on back of a horse, it ain't worth doin."

"Maybe you won't always see it that way." The old man grinned and stepped up into the seat of the buckboard. "You get grown and meet yourself a pretty girl, you'll find out one thing you cain't do horseback."

John Russell made a face. He turned Cricket and rode out across the grassland and left the old man laughing, the windmill turning in twilight.

* * *

The baby began to cry. Sara McKenna unbuttoned the top of her blouse and held little Claudia to her breast. She quieted, suckling.

The scent of frijoles cooking with onions and garlic filled the kitchen. At the cookstove Adela Cienfuegos and her elderly mother chatted in Spanish. The women had been preparing for the return of the vaqueros since early that morning. They'd boiled a great pot of menudo and made flour tortillas and Sara had asked Nestor, the old bunkhouse cook, to prepare his specialty of roasted cabrito, suckling goat kid, smoke-seasoned and tender. The barbacoa would soon be ready. The cabritos were still roasting over the pit outside, a mesquite fire raging below.

Sara stepped to the kitchen window. She looked out where the pasture fell away from the hacienda and in the distance she could see John Russell riding through the last pale light.

She remembered when Jubal decided John Russell was old enough to ride alone, her husband so pleased to make a vaquero of the boy.

This spring marked Sara's thirteenth year in Mexico. She spoke the language of the country and she'd proven herself a fine ranch wife, an able mother to John Russell and Claudia. The baby girl had been born last December, the blessing she'd longed for, come at last after a decade of hope and loss. Three small headstones stood on the hill beside the hacienda, shaded under live oaks. Too precious for this world—Sara's stillbirths in the years between John Russell and his sister, three souls in heaven waiting to meet her someday. Well she knew the pain of carrying a false promise, the bitter sorrow of a lifeless birth. Through the long months of her last pregnancy she'd dreaded another stone on the hill. An unspoken self-reproach haunted all her thoughts—what trespass had she committed, unawares, that her womb seemed cursed? She'd wept in relief to see the girl born healthy and strong.

John Russell startled a pair of doves from the grass.

Sara thought back to that day in the orchard. Sitting under the shade, reading while the boy climbed an apple tree. Out of nowhere, he'd said, "Why's everything so bright?" and she glanced up and saw his eyes lose focus, his expression empty. Then John Russell was falling, convulsing on the ground. That was the year without horses. She'd refused to let him ride, worried sick he'd hurt himself in a fall.

Thank God the seizures had stopped. Life out of the saddle crushed John Russell's spirit—and how Jubal had missed working with the boy.

Sara watched at the window. John Russell put Cricket to a fast walk in the gloaming, headed for home. The boy had his mother's red hair and fair skin, but she saw that already he sat the saddle like his father.

* * *

They gathered around the long table in the courtyard while women brought out dishes in the light of lamps hanging from the vigas. A pair of dogs lay in the corner. Their tails sweeping lazy arcs across the cool tiles. A bat passed over, sounding its echo world.

Jubal sat at the head of the table and held his young daughter in his arms. He watched Sara cross the patio with a bottle of wine. He could smell roasted meat and his stomach was greedy for it.

Sara took a seat beside their guest, the strange Apache child who'd limped like Mephibosheth to the table of the feast. The girl sat with her leg resting on an empty chair, pillows propping her ankle.

Sara used a corkscrew on the bottle and popped it open. She smiled at the girl. "You can call me Sara. What's your name?"

The girl shook her head and stared down at her lap.

"She doesn't speak Spanish at all?" Sara asked Jubal.

"If she does," he said, "she's not ready to talk in front of us."

"That's all right. We're in no hurry."

John Russell sat across from the girl. It had been dark when she'd arrived with his father and the vaqueros and only now in the glow of the lamps could he see her clearly. Deep-set eyes. Skin taut over jutting cheekbones. Her long hair was swept back and she wore a costume of hides.

She glanced at him and John Russell looked away. Something unnerving about those eyes. An ancient quality to them, though she appeared only a couple years older than himself. As if their depths contained the sorrow of ages.

So this was an Apache.

"How long's she goin to be with us?" John Russell asked. He spoke English, their custom in the household and whenever he was around old Wesley, though his Spanish was flawless.

"Till her ankle's better," Jubal said. "I thought maybe it was the best thing, let her stay down in the valley a while."

"Of course," Sara said. "We can move a cot into the nursery and Claudia can sleep in our room."

The vaqueros stepped through the entrance to the courtyard. Sara had waited to begin the meal until the men got the cattle into the corral and saw to their horses. Tomorrow they'd drive the herd back to Nácori, but for now they were tired, covered in the dust of the trail, and all they'd eaten since the day before was pinole and machaca. They took their seats at the table and Sara poured the wine.

The girl removed something from the rawhide bag she carried. She placed a deck of leather cards on the table in the candlelight.

John Russell watched, curious.

She laid a card face up before her, engraved with an array of figures and symbols. She glanced at John Russell in a look he couldn't interpret, then cut her eyes away.

She placed a card in front of him.

He had enough time to see the image of a great tree whose root system mirrored its reaching branches—then a man's voice shouted across the courtyard.

"I'm not eating at the same table with one of those damned things."

They all turned. Mora stepped to the end of the table and stared across at Jubal. "Animals eat on the ground," he said. "Let her sit with the dogs."

The girl snatched up the cards.

"You son of a bitch," Hector said. He started to rise, but Jubal motioned him back.

"Collect your saddle," Jubal told Mora, "and the horse that brought you here." He handed the baby over to Sara, then reached and pulled out his wallet and began counting bills. "I'll pay you out for the month. It should keep you drunk a while."

Mora spat on the tiles. "You invite her to your great supper, give her soft pillows for her foot. Don't you understand what she is? Those butchers raped my grandmother and cut her to bloody pieces when my papa was a little boy. He hid and watched it happen."

"That was a long time ago."

"For you maybe. Not so long to us."

Jubal rose from his seat. He stepped toward Mora, keeping his eyes on the man's hands, the knife in its sheath on his belt.

He offered the money. "Take it and go."

"She'll kill your whole family in their sleep. Cut your boy's throat, smother the baby."

"That girl never hurt anybody."

"Not yet."

"Those days are over. You're talking about the past."

They stared at each other. Then Mora reached for the bills and Jubal gripped his hand and pressed hard, pulling the vaquero against him—too close to draw the knife. Mora winced.

"Don't ever tell me again who eats at my table," Jubal whispered. He tightened his hold. "No one decides that but me. Understood?"

Mora hesitated, nodded his head.

Jubal let go and stepped back.

Mora rubbed his hand gripping the money. "Come on, Angel," he said. "We're done here."

The young vaquero sat beside Wesley at the banquet table. He looked up from the food and wine and met his cousin's gaze. Candleflames shone in Angel's eyes.

"Isidro, aren't you hungry?" he asked.

Mora's voice was flat. "I said we're done. Did you go deaf so you'd feel at home with crippled animals and blind old men?"

"Why do you have to say those things?"

"Listen to me—we don't need him. I'm the one who takes care of you. Have you ever needed anything that I didn't make sure you got it? Since you were a boy."

Angel nodded. "You always take care of me."

"Let's go."

The vaquero rose from the table.

"Give him what he earned," Mora said.

Jubal stared. Then took out his wallet again. When Angel stepped up to him, Jubal gave the vaquero his pay and rested a hand on his shoulder. "You don't have to leave with him. You can stay."

"I know," Angel said but turned and walked on.

Mora spat. "The past never dies in this country, gringo." He led Angel away. They left the lighted patio and passed through the gate and stepped of their own accord into the outer dark.

Jubal looked over the remaining vaqueros. "Anybody else with something to say about who eats at my table can join them. Go ahead, speak up."

No one spoke a word.

"Good. Let's eat."

The kitchen door swung open. Adela and Nestor stepped out carrying a large platter, the first of the haunches of young goat dressed with oils and thyme. The smell was wonderful. The dogs rose from the tiles and whined and stared with beggars' eyes. They set the tray on the table and the feast began. They ate the tender cabrito and drank Jubal's wine. Several glasses later Wesley got out his mandolin. "Here's a rebel song for you," he said and played them *By the Rising of the Moon*, followed up with *Whiskey in the Jar*. The Apache girl delighted in the music. After a while she rose and danced a shuffling dance on one foot to the old outlaw's tune.

* * *

That night the girl lay on the soft cot they'd prepared for her in the nursery. She wore a nightgown that was too big for her and stared up at the ceiling. A moth resting on a wooden beam. She watched it a long time, sleepless. The square room felt alien and distressing. Her people held the circle sacred above all shapes and built their wickiups accordingly. These shadowed corners were unsettling. Wrong somehow.

She lay on the cot and sleep wouldn't come and after a while she sighed and rose. She gathered the pillow and blanket and took up the crutch they'd given her, placing it under her arm, and moved through the dark house.

In the morning John Russell found her asleep in the courtyard with the dogs at her feet.

He stood watching. Studying that chaos of hair like a black storm on the pillow. An odd face unlike other faces he'd known. He was aware it wasn't the kind of face the world called beautiful, but last night he'd glimpsed a strange beauty there all the same and now he was curious if it remained or where it had gone. Her head was canted slightly to the right. A pulse visible in her neck. Beating slowly just over her collarbones.

She woke and blinked the sleep away and looked up at him. It was then he understood her beauty derived from the trouble in her eyes. The boy turned and bolted away.

* * *

The Bavispe River flowed down through the volcanic labyrinth of the Apaches. What the valley people knew of the sierras was rumor and myth, for they traveled those high passes only in well-armed parties, never lingering.

The Apaches roamed an area of mountains seventy-five miles wide and over two hundred miles long. Colossal peaks towered over barrancas. At the bottom of those steep-walled gorges, the days were almost polar in their brevity. You could stand faltering atop a snowy precipice of nine thousand feet and stare down through clouds into an abyss where parrots lighted on palms in a tropic jungleland and naked Tarahumaras dwelled in caves.

Apaches descended to rustle horses and cattle in Sonora and Chihuahua and the American states of Arizona and New Mexico. Their rancherias lay hidden in a land so wild and savage the Spanish never conquered it. Nor had the Aztec emperors when forgotten tribes hid themselves within those cordons. The People dwelled among the ghosts of the Old Ones, the ancient vanished culture of the Sierra Madre.

The McKenna ranch was situated in the Bavispe River valley several miles north of Nácori Chico in the state of Sonora. Over a thousand head of cattle watered along the river and at various springs and lagunas. The largest ranch in the valley, its eastern portions stretched into the foothills.

The country was still rugged and lonesome in that spring of 1927. Yet the land had once been truly untamed, a wilderness when Jubal's grandfather established the small ranch in the late 1860s. Captain Eli McKenna rode among the undefeated. A thousand Confederate troops, country and cause lost. They'd sat their horses on the Texas shore and watched General Jo Shelby sink his battle flag to a watery grave in the Rio Grande. Stones weighing the banner down, descending with the white plume of the general's hat. Then Shelby booted his horse forward and led his men across the river and up onto the banks of that strange land. In Mexico they pledged their services to Emperor Maximillian as a foreign legion.

When he was an old man and bedfast, the captain would tell Jubal of those days. Planting cotton in Veracruz, fighting clashes with Juaristas. Dancing in the ballroom of Castillo de Miravalle with the Empress Carlota herself. A stolen kiss in a shadowed hall.

When the forces of Benito Juárez threatened her husband's reign, Carlota tasked the bold young rebel with a clandestine mission. Captain McKenna never revealed the precise nature of this enterprise. Not even to his own family. Whatever the undertaking, upon its execution he was awarded a land grant in the remote Bavispe Valley.

At the time he moved his wife and young sons to the grant, they were the only Anglos living in the valley.

Later on Mormon settlers arrived by the dozens. Decades to come, the McKennas would enlarge their holdings. They'd purchase thousands of hectares from Mormons fleeing Mexico on church advice during the revolution. Yet in those first fledgling years the ranch was small and the work endless.

They pitched a tent on the hilltop and set about building the corral and making adobe bricks for the hacienda. The captain's wife was the first to find the tracks. Faint prints where they'd crouched watching. No other sign for days. Then came the night when feral shadows moved on the tent wall like players in a magic lantern show and the McKenna boys hid their faces and the captain stayed his wife's hand on the shotgun. The shadows danced. They heard drumbeats, the chant of a low prayer. After a while the Apaches departed, the gift of a deerskin left outside the tent.

Only once did the captain see them in daylight. He rounded a bend in the river and came upon a ragged pair. An old man with milky eyes and a boy gripping a knife. The wind was wrong and cicadas loud in the trees along the banks, or else they'd have heard him coming. The boy looked at him in sudden terror and grabbed the blind man's hand and they darted into the mesquite, the child leading his elderly charge.

The captain sat his horse. A steer stood drinking from the river, their intended prey. They'd looked half-starved and he thought they must have become separated from their band. He rode up beside the steer and pulled his rifle from its scabbard and levered a round and shot the steer between the eyes. Then he turned his horse and rode off.

The family kept a decades-long peace with the Apaches. Both sides abiding an unspoken truce. Elsewhere the generational violence continued as it had for centuries, blood drawn for blood without end.

The McKennas were not to feel the waste of war until the captain's eldest son died fighting for the revolution in 1911. He left no heir. The old man passed away a year later, heartbroken. The ranch fell to Larkin, his younger son. Larkin McKenna went north on a visit across the border only once in his life and when he returned home, it was with a Texas girl as his bride. Jubal would inherit his parents' southern drawl, though he also spoke an accentless Spanish.

The McKenna name was celebrated throughout the valley. The gente called Jubal their patrón just as they'd called his father before him and he learned to shoulder the burden. Few were the families among them without a tale of the patrón's generosity in a year of bad crops or the señora's visit to a sick household with medicine and words of comfort. Jubal's parents and grandparents were buried on the hill behind a wrought iron fence. He had a sister in El Paso, a brother in California he'd last seen twelve years earlier. They'd wanted no part of that hard land, the only land Jubal loved. Even as children they'd been little more than strangers to him.

Jubal desired nothing greater than to work the pastures his father and grandfather had worked. To live and die in the selfsame house. "Never forget whose son you are," his mother told him growing up.

And he never did.

* * *

Jubal and John Russell rode alongside the river while all about them the land lay veiled in a groundmist. Early morning, the air chill. A breeze rustling stands of carrizo cane on the banks. They passed under palms and hanging willows and there was an easy silence between them, father and son.

Jubal halted in the trail. He dismounted and kneeled over a set of prints.

"Lion tracks. Maybe a day old."

John Russell got down off Cricket and crouched beside him.

His father pointed to the front paws. "It's a male. They're spread farther than the hindfeet. Shoulders are broader than the hips, so you know it's not female. Some trackers, they could tell you if he's young or old or big for his age."

The prints were wet under the dew. John Russell studied them. "How can they know all that?"

"Beats me. I was never that good a tracker. Old Mr.

Ballard could tell you everything there was to know without even gettin off his horse. One time he was huntin a mountain lion for us, back when your granddad was still alive. This lion would jump on a cow and kill it, drag it off and take a few bites, then leave the carcass for a vaquero to find. Like it was showin how much it thought of us. We went and got Asa Ballard and took him out to some fresh tracks. He told us it was female, young and pregnant with cubs. Mr. Ballard trailed her through brush and across a bed of rocks where I couldn't see how anything could leave a track. He led us past where she'd killed another calf and straight to where she was holed up. When we found her, she'd already had the cubs."

"He killed her?"

"She roared at us and scared the horses about half to death and Mr. Ballard shot her with his Winchester."

"What'd you do with the cubs?"

"They were yappin away, bawlin for their momma. Your granddad didn't want the job of killin em and neither did I. So we asked Mr. Ballard to do it. What we forgot, years back Ballard found a little cub and raised it full grown. He trained that cub till it was tame as a housecat. Slept at the foot of his bed, if you can believe that. Then one day it wandered out of Ballard's pasture and somebody with a rifle spotted it. The cat made it back to the house, all tore up inside, and Mr. Ballard had to finish it."

Jubal shook his head. "The old man loved that big cat. When we asked him to kill those cubs, he just sat there with the rifle-butt on his leg. Told us he was a tracker, not an executioner. He'd have to charge his goin rate for trackin each one. Otherwise his job was through."

"He didn't want to kill em either."

"None of us did."

"But they had to be."

"Yeah," Jubal said. "They had to be."

"So who finally killed the cubs?"

Jubal rose. "I did," he said and stepped into the stirrup. He swung back into the saddle. "Come on, we better get home. Your momma'll be after me for helpin you play the fox and skip your schoolwork."

* * *

Jubal opened the patio door and stepped into the kitchen. John Russell followed him inside and they tugged their boots off and removed their hats.

"Just in time," Sara told them. "It's almost ready." She stood slapping tortillas from the masa and laying them on the comal to cook.

"I'm fixin to starve to death," John Russell said. He tossed his hat on a peg mounted to the wall.

The Apache girl sat at the table, Claudia in her arms. The baby stirred and began to cry, but the girl rocked her and she quieted.

"You've got a way with her," Jubal said, switching to Spanish. "She won't let too many people hold her without crying. Her name's Claudia."

The girl nodded and made no other reply. None of them could persuade her to reveal so much as her own name. Whenever Jubal asked what she was called, she'd pretend not to understand, or she'd respond with questions in Apache.

She gave them a shy grin and sat rocking the baby.

Sara watched from the comal. "Those eyes. Even when she's happy she looks sad."

"Our lady of sorrows," Jubal said.

And so they called her Dolores.

* * *

It was the practice of that country for Apache captives to work as household servants. Often hard-used, treated as slaves. Instead the McKennas accepted the girl as though she were blood. They gave her no chores and she had free run of the house and ranch and when it was understood she preferred sleeping outside, they fixed a cot for her in the courtyard.

She sat on the split-rail fence of the corral beside John Russell. They watched the jinete at work with a string of frantic mustangs. The breaker had side-hobbled them to their hackamores and all that morning they'd stood tied. Now he led the first of them into the corral.

The mare's eyes were flashing, her ears back, but she didn't try to rear.

A vaquero hobbled her frontlegs together while the jinete spoke soothing phrases and rubbed her neck and chest. He spoke constantly to her. When he thought she was ready, he got the blanket and draped it over her back. He stroked the mare. Then he bent down and lifted the saddle and set it in place.

The girl and John Russell could smell the sweat of her lathered body. Wildness in the air. The mustang stood trembling, breath blowing in and out of her nostrils, and the jinete buckled the cinch-strap. He mounted. The mare snorted and kicked, but the jinete knew what he was doing and reined her hard and the green-broke horse obeyed.

John Russell motioned to a dapple gray that stood sixteen hands. "Now that one there is a hell of a horse," he said. It didn't matter if the girl understood—he could speak endlessly of the horses he loved so well. "But we'll have to get him around cattle to see if he's got cow-sense. You can't teach cow-sense. They either got it or they don't."

The girl nodded to everything John Russell told her. Rarely did she smile. Her eyes were always watching, brimmed with a kind of solemn knowing. As though she perceived dark portent in ordinary events, careless gestures.

She was a long time breaking her silence, but at last

one day at the corral she turned to John Russell. In a Spanish of strange intonation, she said, "I like the look of that mustang with the blazed face."

John Russell flashed her a pleased grin.

From that time on, Dolores spoke freely with them. Her Spanish was often indifferent regarding tense so that it was difficult to tell whether she meant the past, present, or future. In earlier times her people had known the language well, but these bronco Apaches were too cut-off, too isolated in their remote strongholds. The McKennas helped her with the grammar and soon she spoke an excellent Spanish.

Mornings she sang her prayers. She explained them to Jubal and Sara, how she thanked Ussen, the Creator, for their kindness to her. Of her life in those high reaches she volunteered little.

* * *

One afternoon playing in the orchard, John Russell pointed to her rawhide bag and asked to see the card she'd placed before him at the supper. Dolores refused. No matter how he pled she wouldn't let him look on the cards. The boy was angry with her all that day, then afterwards it was forgiven.

* * *

Days passed into months. Among the vaqueros, Dolores was a great favorite and the men always found time to joke with her or play some prank. She teased laughter from Claudia and sang her Apache lullabies and it was plain to see that Dolores loved the little girl. Her ankle was slow to heal, but finally she no longer needed the crutch. She rode the pastures with John Russell, putting their horses to a gallop until they were lathered and dripping and the race decided.

Sara made her a gingham dress. They began lessons with the alphabet and before long she was reading simple words. After a while she stopped sleeping outdoors, comfortable in a soft bed in the square room.

For all the world she seemed content. Yet there was a lonesomeness about her which never ceased.

In early winter she lay awake nights with her people heavy on her heart. Snow blanketed the high country. She was warm down in the valley and it was easier in many ways than her old life. Safer for a certainty. She remembered her mother's hands before she'd lost their touch forever, so big and callused, worn from the constant work of tanning hides. Mexicans had killed both her parents in Chihuahua three years earlier, the orphaned girl raised by her sister and Gouyen the wise woman.

She desired to camp and work in the places familiar to their memory. To follow the paths their feet had worn, to kneel and drink from the selfsame springs. She pined for the mountains of her kinsmen.

Finally the longing was too much to bear.

One evening she came to Jubal in his study where he sat in the rawhide chair behind his desk, leafing through a tally book. The deerskin rug on the floor. A great number of volumes filling the shelves. Leather-bound copies of *The Iliad* and *The Odyssey* in Pope's translation. Stendhal, Balzac, and Dostoyevsky alongside the Barsoom tales of Edgar Rice Burroughs.

He glanced up and saw her there in the doorway. "Everything all right?"

"I need my mule," she said. "My people will be camped in the hills, come down to escape the cold. I have to go to them."

He set the book aside. "Wait a year. That's not so long. Then you can go, if it's what you still want. You could teach them, Dolores. Think of everything you could learn in a year and what you could do for them."

"I have to go."

"John Russell and Sara will miss you. Claudia will miss you."

"And I'll miss all of you," she told him.

There was a silence. Then he said, "You won't stay."

Not a question, just acceptance.

"I can't," Dolores said.

"The mule can carry a pack. I'll give you a horse and rifle, enough food and ammo. But I wish you wouldn't do this."

She said there was nothing for it, she had no choice.

* * *

She rode out on January 2nd, 1928. The morning was cold when they gathered at the gate. Hunched in their coats, the women with rebozos over their heads, breath pluming in the air while they said goodbye. She went down the line of vaqueros and hugged each in turn and then she stood before Jubal.

"You'll always have a home here," he told her.

"I know."

He held her a moment and stepped back, then Sara wrapped her arms around her, the señora fighting to hold in tears and losing the battle. Finally Dolores embraced John Russell and slipped something into his pocket.

When the last goodbyes were said, she climbed into the saddle. He'd given her the bay with the blazed face she admired. She put the horse forward and leading the packmule she passed through the gate and began the return to her mother the mountains. John Russell and his father watched her out of sight beyond the orchard. The boy put his hands in his pockets to warm them and found the little flute.

CHAPTER THREE

She rode cerros timbered with pine and live oak and she rode under dark escarpments of bald granite, her coat tight about her. When frost melted in the afternoons, the ground was treacherous, mud and carpets of pine-needles slick and deadly.

She rode on. Canyon and ridge, foothill and rincon. Meadows where no birds sang and all was windless silence. As though she were a pre-Adamic soul wandering the waste and void in that age before the spirit moved on the face of the deep.

Camping at night she built a pair of fires and allowed the lee fire to burn out. Over its glowing ashes she spread a layer of dirt and placed her bedroll on top. Then she added fuel to the other fire and fell asleep in its warmth.

Late the third day, she felt she was being watched.

She rode on and camped at nightfall and took no special precautions. Her own people were the most dangerous inhabitants of those mountains and what fear did she harbor of them?

The next morning a solitary rider sat his pony on the slope above her camp. She recognized Carnoviste. She raised her hand and the chief turned his horse and set out. The girl unhobbled the bay and mule, then followed at a distance.

After a while they came to the opening of a cave high on the valley wall. Carnoviste dismounted and led his pony through the shadowed entrance.

Her horse was already shying, flaring its nostrils. It wanted nothing to do with the denizens of that place. She got down and staked the bay and mule.

When she stepped through the maw, she was blind a moment, then her eyes adjusted and she saw them huddled on the stone floor in blankets and robes. Like a tribe of cavefolk frozen in ash and time. As though caught unawares by the volcanic upheaval that had formed those heights.

They watched her. Staring at her heavy coat, her jeans and booted feet. No one offered a greeting. Not even Ishton, her older sister who was Carnoviste's wife.

The gray-haired woman she thought of as her grandmother rose with a dark fleece about her shoulders. "Why have you come?" Gouyen asked.

She hesitated. She could hear the strike of hooves on rock in the far reaches. The dank smell of animals and unwashed bodies was very strong.

"I desire my people," the girl said. "I desire to live as they live."

"And die the same death?"

"Yes."

Carnoviste spoke. "This is no place for you. The Mexicans hunt our camps. Not many warriors are left to protect the women and little ones."

"Let me help."

"This life is a hard thing," Carnoviste said. "Daughter, look what you've become. Go home."

She stared at Gouyen with pleading eyes, but the old woman looked away. She kneeled before them, the cave floor cold under her knees. "Forgive what you think I've done," she said.

"Go back to them," Carnoviste told her.

"No. I'm of the People."

Gouyen stepped forward, pulling a knife from her moccasin. She gripped a fistful of the girl's hair and pressed the blade to her throat and looked her directly in the eyes.

"Time is born with a caul on its face," the wise woman said. "What was to be is not and what was not is now to be. The girl you were is lost to us and these mountains have nothing to offer you but death. You're of the valley now."

"I'm not of them."

"Then of the wind. If you ever come into the Blue Mountains again, I'll kill you myself."

Gouyen lowered the knife and turned away.

"I'm Bui," the girl said to her grandmother's back.

"You know me, I'm not a stranger."

Her voice echoed in barren stone. Gouyen paused as though she'd glance back, then found some greater resolve within and stepped into darkness.

"Always our eyes were watching," Carnoviste said. "We saw you were safe, we saw you'd found a place with them. So we knew what must be."

Without another word Carnoviste followed the wise woman.

Dolores kneeled a long time waiting for a moment that would never come. At last she rose from their silence. She stepped out once more into the harsh light and she didn't look back. She walked down the slope and pulled the picket pins and mounted the bay. She rode under exile irrevocable. From where the sun stood at its noonday meridian, the high country was her home no more forever.

* * *

Evenings they'd gather on the porch that wrapped around the adobe hacienda, Jubal fingerpicking his guitar while Sara sang the old songs. The forlorn beauty of her *Barbara Allen* was known to move hard men to tears. John Russell plucked his Jew's harp. His mother's voice drifted through the trees below, Sara singing *Lord Edward* or *Nottamun Town*, ballads out of Appalachian hollows and beforetimes the highlands of Caledonia, melodies carried over the sea and centuries.

They were mad for music, these McKennas. They sang the corridos of the country as well, tales immortalizing racehorses and doomed lovers and outlaws turned revolutionaries. Most nights, if he wasn't in his cups, old Wesley joined them with his mandolin. Their harmonies could alter entirely the feel of a room and there were moments when another voice was discernable among their own, conjured out of vocal unity as though a spirit joined them.

One evening strumming a minor chord, Jubal looked down the orchard road and saw her in the far distance. Lone rider crossing open pasture. No more than a dot on the horizon, but he knew she was returned to the lowlands.

He didn't wait. He set aside his instrument and went down the porch steps and walked out to meet her. When she passed the gate in the twilight, he was there to take her reins.

* * *

By spring round-up at the end of April everyone was too busy to concern themselves with Apaches. Vaqueros set up camps on either side of the ranch and every day they were moving droves of cattle into the corrals for branding and castration.

The sun warmed her face and arms when Dolores rode

out. The distant chain of mountains stood shadowed under a cloudbank, but over her path the sky was clear. She started up a hill where redwings chittered in the boughs of poplar and oak.

At the crest she reined in the bay and sat looking out over the river gorge and the mesa called the Corral de los Indios protruding like a frying pan. A narrow panhandle connected the mesa to the pasture. Decades earlier Apaches had used that mesa as a natural corral to hold stolen cattle before driving them into the sierras. A yearling bucked and galloped. The breeze billowed over the grass and smoke from branding fires climbed the sky.

Dolores lingered among the oaks. She was aware of a subtle shift in the atmosphere, the day gone disjointed of a sudden. Something awry, though what it might have been she couldn't articulate even to herself. She looked down and studied the floor of the grove. As if a message were encoded therein. Nothing to be seen, nothing out of place—then she detected the scent, ever so faint, and knew what sparked her misgiving.

Dolores clapped her legs against the bay's sides. She crossed the pasture out to the mesa's panhandle. She dismounted and opened the gate and led the horse through by the reins and closed the gate behind her and swung back up.

Jubal watched her ride into camp. He stood holding an iron in the fire. A vaquero rode up, stringing along a calf, and Jubal turned to the task at hand.

John Russell removed the catch rope from the calf's neck, then the boy and another vaquero flipped the calf on its side and held its legs and neck. Jubal took the iron from the coals. He pressed the brand to the calf's hide and the iron steamed, the calf lowing, struggling to break free, and Jubal pulled the iron away. John Russell and the vaquero let go.

The calf got up and walked away, the McKenna brand emblazoned on its haunch.

Jubal set the iron back in the fire. The coals pulsed redly. Dolores climbed down and stepped toward him.

He pushed back the short brim of his stockman's hat. "Good day for riding."

She handed him his tobacco pouch. "You forgot it this morning."

He pocketed the tobacco and thanked her.

They were ready with another calf. Dolores stared into the coals while they applied the brand. Once again the calf rose and went on its way.

"What's wrong?" Jubal asked, turning back to her.

She shook her head.

"Something's bothering you."

"They were up there," she told him.

"Where?"

She motioned across the grassland to the hill. "In the trees."

He squatted and opened the tobacco pouch and began

rolling a cigarette. He told John Russell and the vaquero to take a rest.

"You're sure it was them?" he asked.

She nodded. "They hid in the trees and watched you working."

He picked up the iron and touched the red-hot brand to the tip of the cigarette and lit it. He took a long drag. "How many?"

"I don't know. I didn't see their tracks."

"Then what did you see?"

"Nothing. I could smell where they'd been hiding."

He rose. "Show me," he said.

* * *

Searching the hillside, looking for places where the grass was bent or broken. Any sign, however small. Vain effort—if the Apaches had been there they'd come and gone without leaving a visible trace.

Dolores insisted she could smell them, the lingering scent of the animal fat they used to grease their hair. Jubal smelled nothing unusual. If the odor was there, it was too faint for him to discern.

They stood in the oaks and looked down on the river.

"Are you afraid of them?" he asked.

"I don't know," she said. "Maybe."

"Should you be?"

"They won't hurt me, but they'll try to take your

cattle now. Like you owe it to them."

"If they steal a whole herd, I'd call it a bargain."

She smiled.

Jubal asked, "Are you happy?"

She turned and looked through the branches at the blue range to the east. "Is anybody really?"

"I hope so. You've made me happy."

"How?"

"By being here with us. That day at the spring, I saw you step out and it was like you were my daughter. I know you feel apart, but you have a family here. Try to let this be your home."

"I'll try," she said. She stepped to her horse. "I better get back. Claudia likes me to take her out in the orchard to play in the afternoon."

"She's growing, isn't she?"

"All the time." She stepped into the stirrup.

"Dolores," he said. "Don't go out in the orchard today. Stay in the courtyard, all right?"

"All right."

Jubal stood on the hill and watched her mount up and ride back toward the hacienda. He felt a cool breeze out of the northeast coming down from that lost country. "I knew where you belonged the second I saw you," he said. "Not a doubt in my mind."

* * *

Seasons passed. October drew to a close and still no cattle missing. Nonetheless Dolores remained on edge, troubled after dark. She'd stand motionless in the courtyard and study the call of owls, intent and distrustful.

* * *

"Surely you see the danger in waiting," the priest said. "It must be done soon, for her sake."

"When she's ready," Jubal said, "if that's what Dolores wants, she'll be baptized."

They sat under the shade of the open veranda in front of the rectory. A view of mud streets and adobe huts. Above them the church's whitewashed walls gleamed against the sunlight and in the tower the bell hung engraved with the year 1718. Across the plaza a swaybacked ass drove the pair of great millstones, blindfolded and harnessed to a long pole. Turning countless hours in its traces, hooves wearing a circle in the earth.

It was early November and Jubal had received word the priest desired to speak with him. Sara, Claudia, and John Russell accompanied him to Nácori Chico while Dolores stayed behind at the ranch, the girl still uneasy in the presence of strangers.

"This waiting hazards the soul," Father Ortega said.

"Her soul's just fine, Padre."

They were speaking English at Ortega's insistence. The priest claimed he wished to keep up his proficiency with the language and Jubal was happy to oblige. In truth he suspected it was Ortega's sly way of reminding him that his family would always remain outsiders in the eyes of the priest.

Jubal sipped his glass of wine and watched John Russell where he stood with a circle of boys, laughing and talking, in front of his horse Cricket. He was showing them the fine spade bit that Wesley had given him for his thirteenth birthday a few weeks earlier. It was worked in silver with intricate designs and a silver mouthpiece. Only a finely trained working horse of the right conformation and temperament could be commanded with a spade bit at the hands of a skilled vaquero and for Wesley to have presented the boy with such a gift was a great honor for both horse and rider.

Elsewhere in the village, Sara and Claudia were visiting the home of friends.

"Let me caution you against taking risks with eternity," Ortega went on.

Jubal turned to him. "She's nervous here. Leavin the ranch is hard for Dolores, but I'll talk with her about it. You don't have to worry."

The old priest had kept him the better part of the afternoon, pouring wine and making small talk, inquiring about the cattle business, the health of relatives in the states. At last he came to the point. His concern for

57

Dolores—or as he called her the Niña India—and her eternal soul. She must be baptized, she must receive first communion, for there was no salvation outside the Church.

Now the priest wouldn't let it go. Jubal knew his family's stubborn Protestantism had always galled Ortega—and puzzled the gente, however much they admired their patrón.

Ortega finished his glass. He reached for the bottle and poured another round. "Tell me something. She hasn't been tempted by heathen inclinations, has she?"

"I don't follow you."

"I've heard tales about this wild girl."

"What tales?"

"She's rumored to play demonic tunes on a flute of human bone."

"That's ridiculous."

"They say she stares hours on end at leather cards. As if in a trance. Señor McKenna, you must forbid these pagan practices. Not only will it hinder her adjustment to civilization, but perhaps imperil her salvation itself."

Jubal studied the white-haired man, recalling the village rumors of which the priest was himself subject. Father Ortega's past was whispered throughout the valley. Raised in New Mexico, Ortega in his youth had been a member of the order of Hermanos Penitentes before taking up the cloth.

Jubal was familiar with their dark penance. As a boy

he'd witnessed its demonstration one Good Friday, gone with his mother to visit her parents where they were living in Taos, New Mexico that April. He'd stood on the sidewalk gripping her hand as the order marched forth three hundred strong. The brothers bare-chested, wearing capes and hoods. Scourging themselves with short whips. Naked feet left bloody tracks. Some dragged maderos or heavy crosses in the wake of the main procession and there followed a carreta with a wooden skeleton in the likeness of death itself pointing an arrow and stretched bow, the wagon drawn by rawhide cords tied to the ankles of the penitents. A throng shook tambourines and sang hymns. Young Jubal turned and hid his face in his mother's skirt. "Isn't it marvelous?" a woman said, a tourist with an eastern accent and tone of awe. "They perform the crucifixion outside town. Every year one of them is tied to a cross and they raise him up. Isn't it just marvelous?"

The memory chilled Jubal to the bone. Never had he seen a more miserable sight nor yet a graver affront to the Gospel of grace.

"You should know better, Padre," Jubal said. "Rumors can't be trusted. Let me ask you somethin. You really believe God would damn her for not belongin to your Church? The Apostle Paul wouldn't even commit the heathen to hell. He left them in God's hands."

"Communion with God outside the Church is impossible, my son. It's the Church's duty to make us

Christian—on the day of baptism, then in the course of catechesis and so on."

"And the ones who die unbaptized, what about them? My baby girl hasn't been sprinkled. Would she spend eternity in limbo, still too young and innocent to have done anything wrong?"

"You deny original sin, Señor McKenna?"

"Of course not. All you got to do is look at the world."

The priest nodded. "Then if you truly care for your children, bring them into the Church."

He stared at Ortega. "I'm tryin to understand you, Padre. I really am. Maybe it's because you priests never marry, never have kids of your own." Jubal motioned to John Russell playing with the other boys. "You think I could ever reject him, no matter what he did? He'll always be my son. God can't love His children any less."

"Reject the truth if you wish, but the Apache girl doesn't share your disdain. She understands the danger of her situation."

"You talked with her?" Jubal was surprised. Dolores had visited Nácori with the McKennas only once, on Carnival when all the village engaged in revelry and masquerade, but he hadn't known she'd spoken with the priest. Now he recalled the journey home, the girl more somber than usual, her mind turning something over.

"I had occasion to share my concerns," the priest said. "She was receptive."

"What'd you say to her?"

"The truth which remains true despite your protest."

"What did you say to her, old man?"

The priest's eyes flashed. "I told her unless she wishes to burn eternally she must bind herself to the Church. I informed her of the horror awaiting every heathen soul."

Jubal felt the anger rising from deep in his gut. "Listen to me, Padre. I know rumors too. I hear the ones about the shack where you go at night and strip off your clothes. You lash yourself with a whip, put rocks in your shoes and march from one wall to the other, back and forth in that little shack. They hear you cryin in there sometimes. Then come mornin, you clean the blood off and go say mass."

"Señor McKenna—"

"First time I heard about it, I was sorry for you. Sorry anybody believed they were shameful enough they had to torture themselves. But now I understand. You don't whip yourself because you think you're worse than other men. You believe it makes you holier than the rest of us—that's why you do it. So much pride in your own sufferin you scorn His grace. You think mortification pleases God? It fills Him with nothin but grief."

Father Ortega's gaze burned with outrage.

Jubal rose and took his suit jacket from the chairback and shrugged it on. He gripped his hat in his hand. "Never speak to her when I'm not there. You understand me? Never again."

Then he turned from the priest and stepped out into the street and called to John Russell.

* * *

On the long ride home they stopped to eat supper in a valley north of the village. In this valley there was a narrow bed of clay stretching a mile and a half and at the edge of the clay the ancient tusk of a mammoth. John Russell stood over it holding Claudia's hand. The tusk was six feet long and curved like a crescent moon. The color white as milk. Its core was missing, hollow ivory impacted with clay.

Sara and Jubal watched from the shade of a cottonwood. They'd finished their meal of machaca and sourdough biscuits and peach preserves. Sara had removed her black rebozo and her red hair shone in the dappled light through the leaves. She wore a riding skirt, her custom when they visited Nácori—otherwise, in the saddle around the ranch, she'd wear a pair of jeans.

Sara rested her back against the trunk and Jubal lay with his head in her lap. His jacket draped a low branch and he'd loosened his tie. He closed his eyes.

She ran her fingers through his dark hair.

"What did Padre Ortega want to talk about?" she asked.

"Nothin," he said.

"Must've been somethin to get you so mad."

"What makes you think I'm mad?"

"I can tell your moods by the way you sit your horse."

It was true. When she saw him riding home in the evening, she always knew whether he was in an ill-temper, or if the day had gone well. Over the course of their marriage she'd become expert at reading the way he held himself in the saddle.

"I could see it on the ride out," Sara told him. "He got you worked up. So are you goin to tell me what it was about?"

"We had a difference of opinion."

"Regardin what?"

"A religious question."

"Oh, joy. Which one?"

"If it's a sin to eat an egg that a hen laid on the Sabbath. The whole argument hinged on whether or not the chicken had to work for it. You'd have to follow the chicken around and if it looked like she had to strain any, if she squinted hard or kind of grunted, Padre Ortega took the position you'd be breakin the Sabbath. And I held that the whole issue was insane."

"All right," she said. "Don't tell me then."

"You don't believe we had a theological argument over a chicken?"

"Do you expect me to?" She let impatience creep into her voice.

"Listen, I'll tell you later, okay? Just not now. It's too good a day. Let's don't spoil this."

"It is a nice day," she told him.

The breeze was cool, the sky cloudless. From the spring nearby they could hear the sorrowing of the doves. The afternoon was growing late and they still had some distance to go, but the McKennas lingered under the cottonwoods.

Sara had met Jubal at a dance in Van Horn, this brash young rancher from lawless Mexico, come north to visit his uncle and keep an eye out for Texas girls, much like his own father had done. Weeks of courtship followed. Her father more apprehensive each day. She knew Papa liked Jubal and in many ways the two men were cut from the same cloth. They had the same attitudes about the world and their place in it, but her father would never approve for one reason—Mexico. He was afraid Jubal would carry away his only daughter to that savage country. When Papa broached the subject, Sara dismissed his fears. She'd been around cowboys and ranchers all her life and if she was determined about a single thing, it was that she'd never marry one. She had a good head on her shoulders, she told her father. And she meant it—she wasn't about to be swept off her feet.

They were married on a dusty wagonroad outside town. Jubal and Sara had been riding for the preacher's house when they met him driving his buggy, his wife on the buckboard at his side. Jubal hailed him. They told the preacher what they wanted and he set the brake and climbed out and helped his wife down. Jubal and Sara dismounted. They stood holding their reins. The preacher opened his Bible and read from First Corinthians, his wife serving as witness, and married them there in the road.

That evening they'd stood at the door of her parents' house. Sara's heart pounding, knees going weak. Jubal put his arm around her. "It'll be fine," he told her. "Let's go on in."

The family had just sat down to supper, her father and mother and younger brother Buddy. Sara stood beside Jubal, gripping his arm. "Momma and Papa, Jubal and I got married."

Dead quiet. She'd never seen that particular look on her mother's face. Sara tightened her grip on Jubal's arm like a vise.

Then her father rose. "Well," Papa said. "Y'all best set down and eat. Supper's gettin cold."

And that was all he'd ever spoken on the matter.

In the years since moving to Sonora she'd grown experienced in ways she never imagined. She rode with Jubal and the vaqueros looking for lost cattle. She taught John Russell to read from the Bible and McGuffey's *Eclectic Reader* and she could harness a team of mules or milk a cow or wring a chicken's neck. Ranch life had pushed her out beyond her limits just as her father knew it would, but she'd met every challenge with a strength she hadn't known she possessed. Before he died Papa gave her his favorite pair of spurs. By rights they should've gone to Buddy, her brother now an insurance man in Tulsa. Papa never said it out loud, but Sara understood the quiet pride he felt for who she'd become.

She sat stroking Jubal's hair and watching the children. She wouldn't have traded the life they'd made together for anything in the world.

"Tell me somethin," Jubal said without opening his eyes.

"Like what?"

"Tell me anything."

She thought a moment. "Whatever's done out of love takes place beyond good and evil."

He laughed. "That's somethin, all right. What was that, Nietzsche? I didn't think you cared for him."

"I don't admire all of his philosophy," she said. "But I read the quote somewhere and I've been thinkin about it some. There's truth to it."

"Didn't he end up a droolin idiot? What do you figure it means, anyway?"

"Just that you have to judge things differently when it's done out of love. We're still accountable for our actions, but it's not the same, is it? Not like somethin for power or pride or whatever."

"Who's to say love's the real motive? Could be a disguise. You'd have to know somebody's heart pretty well."

"You'd have to know that," she agreed.

They were silent a time. Then she told him, "She'll be all right, you know. Dolores will be all right."

Jubal sat up. He stared across the bed of clay toward the children and reached for his canteen and unscrewed the cap and took a sip of water.

When Dolores had come with them to the Carnival festivities, everyone felt the tension. The villagers greeted Jubal with honor and thanks as always, but they kept their distance from the Apache girl. None of them treated her with unkindness. They were careful to be polite, but Sara understood it was only due to the McKenna family's position of respect, the debts they were owed, and otherwise the girl might not have fared so well.

Villagers passed down stories of forbearers martyred and scalped, a long history of atrocity and revenge. There were many still living who could recall for themselves such outrages. Nowhere in the valley was it a crime to shoot an Apache on sight. Sun-bleached bones were littered along a number of trails in the foothills, bodies cast aside and left to rot.

Sara didn't wonder at the girl's discomfort among them, why she shied from the village girls her age, why she preferred to stay home at the ranch.

"Maybe the consequences are the same," Jubal said.

He'd surprised her, interrupting her ponderings, and she was confused a moment. "What consequences?" Sara asked.

"Whether it's done for love or anything else, the consequences don't change. Not a difference in this world."

"Then in the next," she said.

He smiled. "Maybe so."

Jubal rose and stepped out onto the clay and waved at the children, then went to where the horses stood in the grass and began unhobbling them.

Sara could see the strain in him, the stiff movement of his shoulders, and she knew what troubled his thoughts. What had troubled them for a long time now. They both loved Dolores and it was clear the girl also cared for them. Yet she would forever remain a stranger in the valley.

* * *

The McKennas crested out on the rise and dismounted. The trail before them ran along a gorge. It was a steep descent with places where the trail was washed out and fell to the talus below. They went on afoot leading the horses by the bridle reins and they went single file.

Jubal led his dun a ways ahead to check the path for anything that might spook the horses. He walked with Claudia asleep in his arms. He'd taken her from his wife at the crest, Sara wanting him to be the one who carried the girl if the horses did spook.

Heading to Nácori that morning they'd come upon

a rattlesnake lying in the trail, sunning itself, portions of its tubular body still numb and inflexible. Jubal had drawn his rifle and stepped forward, levering a round, and blown the snake's head off. He told Sara and John Russell to watch the ground. Where there was one snake there would be another.

The gorge lay to his right. Dense brush at his left, hackberry and scrub mesquite and nopal. A solitary magpie darted from the branches when he approached, the rush of wings breaking the stillness.

John Russell was following behind his mother, leading Cricket, when the squaws burst from the dirt and brush beside the trail. Soil rained off the three Apache women. They rose like resurrected witches and the old hag came running between Sara and John Russell. She raised a dagger above her head. Twigs and leaves clung to her tangled hair, her gnarled face and buckskins filthy, all day hidden under a layer of earth in wait for the family's return.

The other squaws rushed in front of Sara waving knives. They attacked in silence, storming the travelers like sisters of a mute coven. When Sara's horse Oro saw them coming, his eyes went wild.

Sara screamed.

Jubal turned, cradling Claudia with one arm and still holding the reins. He tried to reach for the .30-30 in the saddle-scabbard. There was the heavy crack of a rifleshot and something tugged at his fingers, then the dun reared up, front hooves flailing.

A warrior stood at the top of the trail, back the way they'd come, firing down on them. The whites of his eyes shone from a narrow band of black war paint. A pale scar ran down the side of his face and Jubal recognized Apache Juan from the tales the villagers told. Jubal struggled with the reins and got the dun's head down and tried once more to draw the rifle, but two of his fingers were bloody stubs. The lynx-eyed Apache took his second shot. The bullet hit the horse in the neck and warm blood misted Jubal and his little daughter.

The rifleblast echoed in the gorge. Jubal lost his grip on the reins and the horse charged down the trail.

Apache Juan worked the bolt of his Springfield and the empty shell went flying, spinning through the air, sunlight flashing off brass.

* * *

The spent cartridge tumbled through space.

Sara dodged to the side trying to block the squaws with her horse. Oro was terrified and rearing up, all Sara could do to hold on, then one of them hacked the reins from her hand and they were on her at once, slashing her dress, cutting her arms. The crone rushed up behind her and gripped her long red hair. Sara fought to break her grasp—the Apache crone pulling hard, using all her weight—but then Sara's back arched and she was staring up into the faultless blue. The crone cut her throat from ear to ear.

Jubal watched like a martyr forced to witness abomination.

A huge warrior stood over his son where the boy lay sprawled. A young brave whose face was a mask of red and black stepped up to John Russell's horse and fired a pistol. Cricket shrieked and ran crashing through the mesquite, blood pouring from a headwound.

The crone dragged Sara down and kneeled between her legs. Like a midwife tending some unspeakable birth. She gripped the dagger with both hands, a snarl on her lips, and raised it high and plunged the blade hiltdeep in Sara's belly.

Claudia cried against Jubal's chest. Up the trail the warriors were carrying his son away. Apache Juan, the rifle at his shoulder, stared across the chaos to meet Jubal's eyes—

He pulled the trigger.

* * *

The spent cartridge tumbled through space.

John Russell saw the crone attack his mother. He let go of Cricket's reins and started running at the squaws, ready to fight them off his mother or die in the attempt. Rifleshots on the trail behind him, an Apache firing

71

across at his father and Claudia. He didn't see the pair of warriors racing after him.

When the big Apache slammed into his back, John Russell went down hard. The other warrior, a younger brave, raised a pistol and shot Cricket. The sorrel let out a terrible cry and bolted into the brush.

The warrior jerked John Russell to his feet. He was the biggest Indian the boy ever saw. John Russell struggled against him and the warrior punched him in the belly—he bent over gasping. The Apache rapped the side of his head, John Russell's vision dimming for an instant, then stooped and swung him over his shoulder and started running back up the trail.

* * *

As Apache Juan fired the rifle, Jubal stepped off into the gorge. The slope was steep and he held Claudia tight against him and went sliding on his boot-heels in loose dirt. He reached firm ground and started running crosswise downhill.

He ran so fast he was afraid to slow, momentum alone keeping him from tumbling. Mesquite branches slapped at his legs. Claudia had stopped crying and she was taking great sucking breaths. He heard something hit the ground above and come rolling and he knew without looking that it was his wife's body they'd cast off the rim.

A rock gave way under his boot. He fell on his knees and shielded the girl with his arms, gravel and thorns tearing his pants, then he rolled onto his side and scrambled into a mesquite thicket. He lay still and watched the upper slope through the branches. Sara was sprawled midway down the incline. A bloody smile across her throat. An Apache came into view and made his way down the slope in a zigzag—the same young brave who'd shot Cricket, but now he was no longer armed with a pistol, holding a Springfield rifle instead. He stopped where Sara's body lay and raised the rifle one-handed, pointing the barrel to the sky, and pulled the trigger. He kneeled and took something from a pouch tied about his waist. It was an old scalp, short haired and dark. The Apache held the scalp to Sara's throat, pressing it into the blood. He rose and began climbing back up to the rim.

Jubal realized the final echoing shot and the bloody scalp were for John Russell's sake—they wanted the boy to believe Jubal dead with his mother.

He took a deep breath.

Then screamed his son's name in primal torment.

CHAPTER FOUR

As they carried John Russell away he looked back and saw his father vanish into the gorge—and the rifle barked in the same instant.

The crone rose from his mother's body and motioned to the other squaws. They gripped Sara's arms and legs and stepped to the rim. Her head aloll, eyes vacant. They swung his mother off the rim and into the gorge.

John Russell cursed and kicked in the big man's grasp.

The Apache holding the rifle stepped down to them and clapped the boy across the ear with the heel of his palm. In a daze John Russell noted the scar on the man's face. Apache Juan, last chief of the broncos. The chief spoke something in Apache and threw the Springfield to the young brave, who traded him the pistol. John Russell watched the brave step off the trail and move out of sight on the slope below.

The big warrior carried him up the path at a jog. Apache Juan ran beside them. Their hair was long and loose and war charms hung from rawhide cords about their necks.

When they reached the crest, John Russell heard a rifleshot, muted in the bloodrush, and an echo slowly fading. Then what sounded like his name from very far, but he couldn't be sure.

They ran on. All were silent. They crossed into scrub oak and juniper and the squaws followed behind leading Oro, his mother's horse, the only mount not dead or grievously wounded. After a while they came to a clearing in the woods where a dark-skinned boy not much older than himself kept the horses. A white-haired old man danced a circle, chanting a guttural chant. Above his heart the tattoo of a black star. His face was covered in white paint and crimson stripes so that he wore a fierce countenance. A necklace of bear teeth and claws dangled against his chest and he sported an old buffalo hat. The horns on his head fearsome and evil-looking. He ceased his dancing when he saw them.

They stood talking a moment. The big warrior set John Russell down and they waited. Soon the brave who'd gone down in the gorge emerged into the clearing and tossed the rifle back to Apache Juan. He was holding a dripping scalp and he came over and dropped the black thing at the boy's feet.

The hair was the length and color of his father's and it was covered in fresh blood. John Russell stood staring. He wept without making a sound.

Apache Juan slid his rifle into the sleeve on his saddle. He mounted and motioned for the boy to be handed up.

Then they were riding.

* * *

Jubal rose and held Claudia, the girl crying again. His face and the face of the child were streaked with the dun's blood. His pants were torn, his knees skinned and burning. The index and middle fingers of his right hand were missing at the second knuckles, the stubs still bleeding, and he got out a bandana and wrapped his hand. There was no real pain yet, adrenaline pumping through him.

The sun fell below the ridgeline at Jubal's back and evening stars appeared. He knew they wouldn't have left a horse that could ride, so he climbed down to the bottom of the gorge and started running toward the ranch in the twilight.

By the time he burst through the front door it had been dark over two hours. Dolores looked up from her place by the kerosene lamp and saw him standing there with the girl at his chest, dried blood on their cheeks. She rose to her feet. A look of dread certainty in her eyes.

"They took him," Jubal said.

* * *

In the haste Hector saw to the loading of the packmules. Vaqueros saddled horses and led them out to wait under the stars. They were all armed and ready for the chase. Jubal had promised a reward, but they cared nothing for it—they'd ride for vengeance just as their fathers had once ridden.

Dolores wet a rag and cleaned Claudia's face and stood in the kitchen rocking the exhausted girl to sleep.

Jubal sat at the table pulling on his boots. He wore a mackinaw over a chambray workshirt and jeans. Gauze covered his mutilated fingers. On his hip a holstered Colt 1911 semiautomatic. Boxes of .45 ammunition sat on the table and he dumped one out and started thumbing rounds into spare magazines.

Dolores watched, hesitating. Then she said it—

"You can't go after him."

He looked at her. "What are you talking about? We're going to bring him back."

"You'll get close," she said. "Then they'll kill him. When they know you're close, they'll kill him like they did her. Worse if there's time."

"Listen to yourself. You want me to let the sons of bitches take him for good?"

"I'm asking you. Don't do this."

He swung his hand and swept a pile of rounds from the table. They rained in a clatter of brass and rolled about her feet and Claudia woke and began crying.

"What do you want me to do?" Jubal demanded. "Tell

me what the hell I'm supposed to do."

"They won't give him up. You have to wait. They'll stop watching him when they're sure he won't run. When he has a life with them. But you have to wait."

"He saw them cut her throat. You think he's going to be able to live with those animals after that?"

"He has to. He's got to become one of them if he wants to survive."

"You don't understand what they did out there," he told her. "They have no souls."

"Yes, we do."

"Don't ever talk like that. You're nothing like those gut-eaters."

He shoved the loaded magazines into his pockets and picked up the remaining ammo boxes. "I'm going to find your brother. You'll take care of Claudia?"

"Of course," Dolores said.

"We'll send back a couple men with Sara. They'll bury her on the hill. Anybody gives you trouble, tell them they can talk to me when we get back."

"All right."

"All right," he said. He stepped to the door and opened it.

"Papa?"

He looked back. "Yes."

"I've seen," she said. "I've seen before and I pray to God you don't catch up with him."

They rode out under the blind huntsman, Orion

79

chasing the flock of doves across a black vault to slip beyond the western horizon, Jubal and his riders moving east as if caught up in a counter-current, the heavens at odds with the earth.

* * *

In the long night of riding, John Russell watched for a perfect moment. They'd taken his claspknife and he had nothing to use for a weapon. He studied the trail ahead and planned possible escapes, rejecting one strategy after another.

They rode up hogbacks and slopes of volcanic rubble and down corkscrew trails under the pale light of the moon. From time to time they spoke in hushed Apache, but for the most part they rode in silence. He sat the saddle in front of his captor, every step the horse took carrying him farther from home and rescue.

After leaving the clearing they'd split up, the group that held him heading due east, the other southeast. He rode with the warrior who seemed their leader— from the scar on his face, John Russell knew he was Apache Juan. Only the older Apache with the buffalo horns, the medicine man, commanded a similar degree of respect.

They kept the horses at a fast walk or slow trot where the trails permitted. They were taking pains to confound trackers. Dodging and twisting and turning all directions.

Doubling back like a fox and traversing stretches of bare rock where the hooves, sheathed in their buckskin boots, made no slightest trace. They passed like ghosts.

He looked up at the stars and swayed in the saddle. They were taking him through the foothills high into the sierras, far from where his family lay dead in the valley. They rode on and after a while he knew the perfect moment would never come—their watchfulness wasn't slacking. Everything in him called for action.

When they turned and started up a hillside, John Russell threw himself from the saddle. His shoulder thudded against the ground, the air going out of him, and he started rolling, brambles tearing at his skin. He came to a stop at the base of the hill. He got to his feet and stood reeling and glanced back and there was the chief running down after him.

The other Apaches sat their horses and watched the little chase in amusement. The soles of John Russell's boots were slick and the ground was covered in pine-needles. He could hear them roaring laughter when he fell headlong, his face plowing needles, then Apache Juan overtook him.

John Russell picked up a stone and swung. The chief grabbed his arm and put him in a headlock.

John Russell cursed. "Kill me or turn me loose."

The chief laughed and let go. The boy spat in his face.

Apache Juan wiped the spittle from his smooth jaw, then clouted John Russell across the head. He fell to the ground. The chief offered his hand, but he ignored it and rose.

John Russell smiled his sweetest smile. Apache Juan grinned back. He thought the chief likely spoke Spanish, so he cussed him in English, his tone pleasant as though talking to a dog. "One of these nights, I'm goin to saw your damn head off," he said. "Then swap it for a pile of horseshit. Don't stop grinnin if you think that sounds like fun, you sorry bastard."

They started walking back. The boy went without protest save a string of amiable curses.

* * *

John Russell nodded off in the saddle and jolted awake again and again. His belly growled. He craved sleep second only to food and he eyed the leather packs they carried, but they didn't stop to eat nor did they eat while horseback.

In the hours before dawn they crossed a ridge and came down its eastern flank and met an old wagonroad. It ran above a valley wherein lay the headquarters of a small rancho. A cabin stood by the corral, windows dark, the shake roof weighed down with smooth rounded stones carted from the riverbed. The rocks were pale and strange in the moonlight. As though great mushrooms grew atop the house.

They left the road and descended the valley wall and

crossed through a pasture. Night breeze, cattle grazing. A suckling calf at its mother's teat.

Apache Juan spoke to one of the braves and the brave dismounted and drew a knife from the fold of his moccasin. The calf didn't try to run. When the brave slit the calf's throat, the mother cow bawled. Another warrior dismounted waving his arms and slapped her flank and sent her on her way.

The brave threw down the calf and kneeled. He cut into it and reached and pulled out the heart jumping like a bullfrog in his hand and took a bite of that toothsome organ. The calf's back legs were still kicking. Next he cut the belly open and took the stomach and stabbed it to get at the soured milk contents. He grinned and began drinking the stuff as though it were a rare delicacy.

They all climbed down. Apache Juan dropped to one knee beside the calf. The medicine man limped over and kneeled with him. They removed the liver and pair of small kidneys and devoured them, eating slowly, savoring the taste, and they dined on raw viscera like epicures and gourmands.

John Russell looked away, disgusted at the sight.

The chief made signs for the boy to eat. John Russell shook his head.

"Eat," the chief said in Spanish.

He started to speak, but Apache Juan jerked him down before he could get a word out. He gripped the boy's neck and shoved his face into warm entrails. He took the calf's stomach from the brave and made the boy drink the warm curdled milk inside. John Russell gagged. Apache Juan held the boy's head back and spilled the stomach into his mouth and thick white milk poured on the ground and ran and mixed with the blood of the calf.

John Russell coughed and spat, then the chief wrenched him to his feet. They remounted and set out again.

At sun up they were still riding. They rode all morning and they rode so hard he thought they'd use the horses to death and thereafter compel from the carcasses a posthumous half-mile. Noon found them climbing another jagged ridgeline. All that day they climbed, pausing on occasion to give the horses brief rest, letting them drink at springs that oozed and trickled from stratified conglomerate. Their course had turned northeast, heading into the heights of the sierras.

Their horses wavered on the brink of exhaustion. The Apaches kept pushing, determined to get as much distance out of them as they could.

Late that night they arrived at the rendezvous. Brush and ocotillo stalks barred the entrance to a box canyon. They cleared a path and led the horses through and blocked up the entrance again. John Russell dismounted and stumbled. They walked leading the horses and at last they came to a spring where a young brave waited with mules, fresh mounts.

The squaw who'd accompanied their group unrolled

blankets and handed out a cold supper of mesquite bean meal and dried pounded meat. They were confident of eluding any pursuit but not so foolhardy to risk a fire.

When the squaw was finished, she took from her bag a buckskin shirt, pants, and pair of moccasins. She came and stood over John Russell. She was short and plump and much bigger than the boy. She took hold of him and pulled off his boots. Then she undressed him, tugging his good Sunday jacket free and ripping his shirt open, buttons flying, and she unbuckled his belt and jerked down his pants. The squaw threw his clothes aside.

"Wait," he said. He jumped up and took the bone-flute from the pocket of his suit jacket, the same jacket that was always so hot he couldn't wait to take it off. He looked at the dress pants, the shirt with its too-tight collar, the clothes his mother made him wear when they visited Nácori.

For the first time in his life he wanted to put them back on.

The squaw made him sit. She grabbed his feet, pulled off his socks. Lastly she stripped him of his underwear. When he protested, the squaw seized his ear and twisted it crimson.

He stood naked under her gaze. She handed him the buckskins and moccasins. When he put them on, she looked him over and nodded once and actually giggled. The chief came and led John Russell away. He didn't see what she did with his old clothes.

The chief bound his arms behind him with a rawhide cord, then tied his feet together. He sat beside John Russell and ate his ration and when he'd finished, he took handfuls of mesquite bean meal and fed the boy. It tasted good to him. He was so hungry he didn't care he was being fed by hand like a pet.

The squaw had started to work unsaddling the horses and outfitting the fresh mules. While the braves ate, she hauled heavy saddles and threw them on the backs of the mules and pulled latigos and fastened backcinches. Then one by one she staked the new mounts.

A stand of cottonwoods grew about the spring. The chief rose and went to a deadfall and broke off a long thick branch. He gathered two stout sticks, each forked on one end, and drove them into the ground, leaving six feet of space between them.

"On your belly," he told the boy in Spanish.

He tied John Russell's arms and legs to the branch, then he called to the young brave who'd been waiting there in camp. The brave came and gripped one end of the pole. The chief gripped the other and they lifted John Russell, the boy hanging facedown, rawhide biting into his wrists and ankles. They set the pole in the forks. When John Russell inhaled, his chest almost touched the ground.

He craned his neck and grinned at the chief. "You should've killed me. I'm goin to cut your throat with your own knife, first chance I get."

Apache Juan picked up a heavy rock. He placed it on the small of John Russell's back, then turned and stepped to where the squaw had spread his blanket. He lay down and went straight to sleep.

The brave walked out into the night with a rifle to keep first watch. John Russell hung suspended, sick with hatred and despair. He wanted to cry, but he wouldn't let himself. The cords cut into him. Despite all his exhaustion he thought sleep impossible, but after a while his eyelids eased shut against his will and he did sleep.

* * *

The grave lay open and waiting.

Dolores stood on the hill with the others under the late afternoon sun. In the sky a faint autumnal haze. Oak leaves fell and drifted and a solitary leaf went sailing into the grave.

Old Wesley wore a black armband of mourning. Hector's wife Adela and her mother raised their veils and dabbed at their eyes with handkerchiefs. Outside the wrought-iron fence a small crowd had gathered. Vaqueros from neighboring ranches, mourners from Nácori—the news had spread fast through the valley. Dolores looked for the old priest, but he wasn't there.

She wore a black dress and rebozo, black shoes so well-polished they darkly gleamed. She held Claudia's hand and they watched the vaqueros walking up the hillside, carrying the pine casket.

When the vaqueros stepped through the gate, Adela Cienfuegos crossed herself. They set the casket down. From the grassy slope there was the soft call of a quail.

Women cried, men stood with arms crossed. Wesley stepped forward holding a battered pocket New Testament and opened the book.

Dolores longed for a knife. Her hand burned to close around the grip, to cut her hair and dress and skin, wail until her throat was raw. She wanted to grieve the Apache way, but the crowd was watching.

So Dolores stood in silence among them and discovered that now she couldn't even cry. She tried, but no tears came and she never felt so empty.

Wesley spoke without looking at the page, going from memory.

"Who shall separate us from the love of Christ? Shall tribulation or distress or persecution? Or famine or nakedness or peril or the sword?"

Dolores squeezed the girl's hand.

"My sheep hear my voice and I know them and they follow me," he said. "And I give unto them eternal life and they shall never perish, neither shall any man pluck them out of my hand." He paused and worked his jaw back and forth, the way a man does when he's struggling not to weep. "My Father, which gave them me, is greater than all and no man is able to pluck them out of my Father's hand. I and my Father are one."

Wesley closed the book. He stared out across the grassland.

"When I was stove up a few winters back, Missus McKenna would bring my supper out to the bunkhouse. Her and Mr. McKenna kept me on the place when I should've been put out to pasture. That's just how she was. Took care of folks. Never hurt nobody her whole life, but they killed her anyway and carried off that boy. I ought to've been the one. Can you tell me why a old hell raiser like me is still alive and not her? I don't understand it. But I stopped tryin to figure things out a long time ago."

His tears streamed down to white stubble. He cleared his throat and started to speak and cleared it again.

"I loved to hear her voice on that porch of a evenin, sangin so pretty. About like a angel. Well, now there won't be no more sangin, I reckon, till we all go home together."

Dolores felt a gaze. She glanced over and saw Adela's mother glaring at her behind her dark veil. Dolores looked away.

"All right," Wesley told them. "Go ahead."

The vaqueros lowered the casket down into the grave with their reatas.

Dolores picked up Claudia. She held her, the girl's head resting on her shoulder.

The old woman walked up to Dolores. She leaned on her cane and raised her veil with a trembling hand, gloved in lace, and looked Dolores in the eyes. Then she lowered her head and spat on Dolores's polished black shoes.

"Look what you did," the old woman said. "And not even a tear for her. He should've let them kill you the day they found you."

"Mother, don't," Adela said.

"At least he gave you a true name. You cause nothing but sorrow."

Adela tugged her mother's arm, shaking her head at Dolores in apology. They turned and started down the hill.

Dolores felt the crowd's eyes on her, the mourners blaming a fourteen-year-old girl for all that had occurred, every heart in accusation, and she thought maybe they were right. Better she'd died that day at the spring and this hour never come to pass.

Still she couldn't cry and she wondered how a heart could be so cold.

Then Wesley had his arm around her. "This ain't your fault, darlin. Don't listen to nobody who tells you any different."

"I'm sorry," she said and her voice broke.

"What you got to be sorry for? You ain't done nothin. Let me tell you somethin. That little girl needs you right now—you cain't be so hard on yourself."

Dolores turned her face into the old man's shoulder. She wept into his shirt, holding nothing back. She tried to stop, but sobs choked her throat and the flood kept coming.

"Well, I reckon I'm sorry too," Wesley said. He took a bandana from his pocket. "Dry up. Let's go on back to the house. Keep a holdt of me—you got to be my eyes, or I'm liable to take a misstep and tumble down."

Dolores dried her tears. She took the old man's arm and went guiding him down the hillside.

The vaqueros picked up their shovels. Dirt rained on the pine-box.

A white cross marked the new grave and the shadow of the cross fell on a carpet of dead leaves. The sun lowered in the west and the shadow lengthened, reaching out for the little headstones crowned with resting lambs.

* * *

Painted saints with wooden eyes stared from the make-shift shrine on the table. The santos were gifts of the mourners. Dolores knew they were images of dead people and she couldn't understand why anyone would allow such a thing in their home. Now more than ever the dead were watching.

She stood in the doorway, afraid to enter the kitchen. On the tabletop a candleflame bent and righted as though at the passing of some unseen presence. Adela had lit the votive candle earlier, a prayer for the success of the searchers.

The mourners were gone now, headed back to their villages and farms. After the burial they'd lingered, talking among themselves in low tones, remarking on the disgrace—one of those savages living in the same house. Some expressed the opinion Claudia should be taken to Nácori, cared for by friends of the McKennas. They changed their minds of a sudden when Wesley produced his 12-gauge and made it clear the child wasn't going anywhere.

The candleflame flickered.

Claudia lay asleep in her cradle and otherwise the hacienda was empty. Dolores watched the flame and the pooling wax. There was the scent of roses in the air, very strong, and after a while she realized she was crying again.

She gathered her courage and stepped into the kitchen. Among the myriad icons was a small likeness of the Santo Niño de Atocha. Many in the valley were devotees of the Child Jesus, praying daily for the safekeeping of their family.

Never before had Dolores seen the figure, but something about the image of the child struck her and when she picked it up and looked at the eyes, there was no longer any fear in her.

When she stepped outside, it was cool and the moon shone bright. She took a trowel from Sara's rosebed and walked out of the courtyard.

In the orchard she moved among the rows of trees until she found one greater than all the rest, higher than its fellows so that the trees to each side grew under its shadow. She set the figure down and began digging. She dug a small niche below the tree. Then she placed the santo inside and closed up the opening. She'd no way of knowing, but such was the custom in that country in times of adversity for supplicants of the Christ Child to place His image in captivity.

Dolores stood looking at the moon where it hung over the far mountains. Then she turned and went back to the house and left the santo in its hiding place.

* * *

John Russell woke when the other group rejoined them, entering camp in the dark some hours before sunrise, and he recognized the big Indian who'd carried him on the trail, recognized the old hag who'd killed his mother. The new arrivals ate a quick meal, then slept while the young squaw took care of their horses. The boy hung from the pole, trying to return to sleep, but the night was cold and his teeth chattered and his wrists were bloody and howling.

When dawn reached forth, they untied him.

Puss ran from sores about his wrists. He got to his knees. He tried to stand and dropped back down. He sat working his fingers back and forth, everything aching, and his weariness amazed him.

He rubbed his wounds a while, then stumbled out into the brush and relieved himself.

At the spring the squaws kneeled filling canteens. The boy walked to the pool and took off his moccasins. When he plunged his feet and ankles under the water, pain stung him, but he refused to show it. He bent and washed the sores and raw skin around his wrists.

His respite was short lived. They mounted up and rode out leading yesterday's horses. The boy was dead in the saddle and his captors hadn't managed much rest themselves, but the Apaches refused to slow their pace.

The big Indian led his mother's horse Oro. John Russell looked away from the empty saddle. The hag rode with them now, her long hair loose and gray, obscuring her face, and the boy watched her as they rode and nursed his hate.

* * *

To the north raincurtains lowered over the cordilleras. Distant chains of serrated peaks pierced ashcolored sky. It was raining in the Sierra Madre where they were bound and come nightfall rain would turn to snow.

The Apaches watered the mounts at the river and crossed over. Mules and horses splashed through the little stream. The water was a foot deep, flowing clear and rapid through the valley between the two ranges, and they rode up onto the banks and took a trail following the stream for some distance.

John Russell wanted to lie in the cool water, let it wash over him. In the sierras temperatures swung between extremes. It was well over a hundred degrees now at late afternoon, but when they camped that night in the higher elevations, it would fall below freezing.

They rode among palms, the last of their kind to be seen where they were going, and the mules trod thick bambusa, pale green contrasting darker shades of oaks. Blue jays nested in the boughs of small pines.

The Sierra Madre rose bold and fearsome and waiting millennia long to accept him into her mystery. Ascending a cordon which led up to the main cordillera, they were obliged to get down and lead the mules along the steeper slopes. Fallen rocks littered the trail and boulders clung to the mountainside above.

Finally when they camped that night in the cold and the pines, the chief didn't tie him to another pole. Instead his hands were bound behind his back and his feet bound and the chief bent his knees and lashed the cords together. John Russell lay hogtied. The chief spread a blanket over him, then lay down and closed his eyes.

The boy knew their rest would be short. He worked the rawhide knots, then heard footsteps and went motionless. The watchman's relief walked past. John

Russell struggled with the cords, flexing and pulling, but he was bone-weary and nodding off and rousing himself and at last he nodded off and didn't rouse.

Lying awake beside the boy, Carnoviste the war chief watched him fall to sleep's kindness.

* * *

"Somebody was waiting for them to swing back this way," Hector said. He cursed. "The sign was getting cold fast enough, now they got fresh mounts."

"We'll ride harder," Jubal said. He stood under the cottonwoods at the edge of the pool.

"Nobody's waiting for us with fresh horses."

Jubal kneeled and studied the prints in the sand. Hooves shod in strips of rawhide. Muddled tracks of animals who watered at the spring, coyotes and woodmice and a doe with her fawn at her side. Within that network of sign he could see the prints of small human feet leading toward the pool before they merged with the tracks of the beasts. He stared at the impression of a bare foot the size of his son's. A coyote had stepped on the last print where it met the water.

He pressed his palm to the impression and held it there. Then he rose and waved for the men to lead the horses up. "Let them drink," Jubal said.

He faced Hector. "You want to go back? Turn around and go home."

"You know I'm with you. But the sons of bitches are losing us every step."

"They can't run forever."

Jubal had led them back to the site of the ambush and he'd wrapped Sara's body in a blanket and carried her up the slope, refusing to let the others help, then two vaqueros were left behind to bring her home. Hector had found Cricket, John Russell's horse, dead in the mesquite in a pool of blood. He'd taken the spade bit from the sorrel's mouth and placed it in Jubal's saddlebag. They'd trailed the Apaches by the light of a full moon and they'd kneeled with a lantern over the ground where the tracks diverged. The horses wore rawhide boots, all except one—and he recognized these tracks. It was Sara's horse Oro. They followed the group with his wife's mount, pursuing southeast up the hogbacks, and came to where the Apaches had paused to boot Oro's hooves.

Soon they lost the trail altogether and they were a long time picking it up again. Then once more in the night they lost them and Jubal circled and cut for sign and found nothing.

Finally they had to give up and wait for first light. A supper of jerked beef and cold tortillas. Afterward the vaqueros slept. Jubal lay awake, his mind in seething turmoil, sharp throbs of pain in the stubs of his mutilated fingers. At dawn he was walking over the ground looking for sign.

In the morning light they tracked them through dense thickets of oaks, down hills eroded with gashes seaming the rock in all directions, and up arroyos whose slopes held the stone walls of the ancients' terraced gardens. After a while the tracks turned north and climbed into the foothills. Century plants rose on stalks twice the height of the horses. Nopal and mesquite and maidenhair fern threatened to reclaim the faint footpaths and game trails.

The following night cost them more time they couldn't afford to lose. Then the next day they'd come to where the tracks of the two parties reunited, one set hours older than the other, and trailed them to the spring in the canyon.

Now the Apaches were riding fresh mounts. Jubal knew there was no overtaking them, but he wasn't going to turn back.

* * *

Jubal and Hector rode out ahead.

The sky gray as a leper's shroud, rain obliterating the tracks. They came down the slope with raindrops pelting their slickers and they entered the valley. Between the two sierras flowed a little river called the Huehuerachi after the mountains they'd just quit.

They drew up at the stream, got down, and let the horses drink. In the twilight and the rain they waited for the vaqueros to catch up.

The opposite bank was mud and puddles and no more trail to follow. Beyond the river barren-looking hills of solidified volcanic ash. Beyond them, in turn, the towering Sierra de Nácori—part of the Sierra Madre proper, cut off by the upper Bavispe, the river making its great detour from its headwaters toward the north around the range. The mountains loomed close. As though a quake would send them crumbling down to bury the valley.

"He's a strong boy," Hector said. "John Russell's not the giving up kind."

Rain streamed off Jubal's hat brim. "I know. We're not giving up either. We keep going."

"The tracks are gone. There's no more sign."

"Then we don't have to wait for first light. Move fast, close the distance."

"We don't have supplies," Hector said. "Not enough to be up there so long. They could be anywhere in those mountains."

"I'm not going home without him."

They crossed the river in the dark and traversed the woodland cordon. Riding where beforetimes none of their number had set foot. Most of the vaqueros were farther from their valley home than ever in their lives.

The tracks were washed away, nothing to go by. The horses took sucking steps through the mud and they had to lead them afoot on the slopes and by midnight they'd made little progress.

Wrapped in coats and slickers they longed for return of the day's warmth, the heat they'd spent all afternoon cursing. Snow fell. Crystals descending out of the dark void, clinging to pine-needles.

Pale dervish spirits rose whirling from drifts of snow and stung Jubal's cheeks. He was almost glad the sign was destroyed, nights of waiting ended, now drive on without rest or regard for the horses. He hoped for arrogance, the Apaches so confident of their lead they'd shelter and wait out the storm. He didn't know how he was going to find them, but he was determined to.

Jubal dismounted. He drew his Bowie knife and went to a sapling and cut a forked branch, still green on the inside. Then he sheathed his blade and walked off alone. Holding the branch out before him by either fork he turned a slow circle in the snow. He could feel it bending in his grip. The bark beginning to peel away. He could see the branch curving out to the side and he turned in the direction it wished to go and the branch straightened again. Jubal went striding back through the snow and returned to the men. "I know the way," he told them. And so they set out again.

They led the horses up a trail running between a sheer wall of granite and a straight drop. In the lead Jubal came to where the trail was washed-out and bridged by a narrow ledge. He stood looking down at snow spiraling into oblivion.

Too far to turn back and circle around. They were hemorrhaging time.

Jubal got his blanket and wrapped it about the horse's head. He led the horse by the reins and stepped out onto the shelf. Once and only once did he glance downward. He snapped his gaze back up of a hurry and kept his eyes forward, then he was on the other side.

"It's safe," he shouted at the others. "Come on."

Hector made the sign of the cross and covered his horse's head. He drew on his cigarette. The tip glowed redly. He stepped out on the ledge and flicked the butt away and smoldering ash spun and vanished out of sight.

When he'd made it, Hector looked back and shook his head grinning. Jubal clapped his shoulders. They waved for the next man. The vaqueros went, bringing their horses across, taking turns going back for the packmules, then finally the last man reached the end and spat. "Hijo de la chingada," he cursed.

The snow abated and dawn bloodied the sierras to the east. Spread out before them were successions of pine-covered plateaus and hills. Three inches of snow had fallen during the night and where the mesas were open and parklike, the rising sun coppered those pale blankets. They remounted and set out up the side of a ridge. Jubal startled a hawk feasting on a dead rabbit in the trail and the hawk beat its wings and rose gripping its prey.

Strange monuments of uncut stones. Heaped three

feet high, several in a line running east to west. The vaqueros wondered at their meaning—shrines, perhaps.

Refugios, Hector told them. They were crude defensive walls and shooting stands. Apaches built them on a hillside to fend off pursuit along the trail below. "Look close," he said. "You'll see old casings."

The vaqueros looked. At the foot of a refugio they spotted brass Winchester casings, remnants of forgotten battles.

By mid-afternoon the snow was melting and the ground thawed and turned to muck. They got down again and led the horses. Boots caked in mud, heavy on their feet. The vaqueros argued among themselves which was the rougher going, snow or mire. They walked pine shadows where snow lay yet and they tracked through it bespoiling the pure white canvas. Ice fell from the undersides of pine boughs and great crackings echoed in the woods.

That night no further snow fell. The ground hardened in the freeze and they kept going with little rest to speak of.

Hector stepped up beside Jubal. "We've covered a lot of ground. What do you say we stop a while, give them a break?"

Jubal shook his head.

"You're a hard man, my friend," Hector said. "Maybe you can keep going forever, but the boys are dead on their feet. How much longer?"

"We'll rest when we've got him back."

* * *

Not until they reached the crest of the sierra and looked down on the falling away of almost three thousand feet did they at last feel an eastern wind. Deep in the pine region. Forests so dense they allowed no view of the woodland floor. A lone hawk wheeled below.

Jubal led them forth into latterday Apacheria.

Wandering without fixed path, without certain direction, keeping generally to the north. From time to time Jubal would get down and stalk off away from the men and consult his branch. When he mounted back up, he'd make some small correction to their course and keep pushing them onward. Hector was alarmed to hear the patrón muttering to himself as they rode. He studied his old friend. Bloodshot eyes, manic expression. Jubal hadn't slept in almost two days. Before that what little sleep he'd managed was fitful, tortured by nightmare. How far could a man push himself?

The lightning-struck tree stood at the summit of a rocky upthrust. Jubal broke away, putting his horse to a trot, and climbed the slope. Under the blackened skeleton he halted and again dismounted and surveyed the country. He produced the branch from his saddlebags and slowly turned on the rock, but there was nothing, all lost, no longer a sense of invisible energy flowing through his hands. As though the branch had stopped speaking to him of a sudden, a greater magic at work in those ancient heights. He cursed and snapped the branch in two and cast the broken sticks away.

He waved for Hector. The segundo started up the rise. They stood side by side.

"You brought the mirrors?" Jubal asked.

"In my saddlebag," Hector said.

"Pick the two best trackers. The three of you head out in separate directions, cut for sign."

"They're not going to like that. Riding alone. Not in these mountains."

"They don't have to like it, they just have to do it."

"You sure about that?" Hector shook his head. "I think you'd better talk to them yourself. Explain what you're asking here."

Jubal stared at him, then nodded.

Hector shouted down to the vaqueros. "Cruz, Medina."

The pair booted their horses. When they reached the top, Jubal kept his gaze on the far terrain. "We need to scout for sign," he told them. "Each man goes by himself. I'm not giving you an order, you're not in the army. You can tell me to go to hell, but I need your help."

He turned and looked at Medina and Cruz, then his eyes settled on Hector and held there. "I'm asking you to do this for me. Help me find my son."

The vaqueros hesitated.

"I'll go," Hector said.

"Thank you."

"I know you'd do the same if it was my boy."

"All right, Patrón," Cruz said. "Me too."

Medina nodded as well.

Hector retrieved the small mirrors from his saddlebag. He passed them to the vaqueros and kept one for himself. They'd use the looking glasses to signal the main party, just as General Miles's cavalry had employed the heliograph in those same mountains decades earlier.

"So many damn trees," Medina said. "How are we supposed to signal?"

"Get to a high place," Jubal told him. "I'll be watching. If you don't find anything in a few hours, don't push it. Leave yourself enough time to get back here by dark."

"This is crazy, what we're doing," Medina said. "Who knows how many of them are out there?"

"Go with God," Hector said. "And don't let them take you alive."

Hector remounted and turned his horse and rode back down the incline. The scouts followed after him, then each man split away and went alone into the wilderness.

A vaquero walked up the broken hillside to take Jubal's horse. He led it down to where the men were picketing their mounts and placing morrals over their heads, letting them eat a ration of grain.

Jubal stood alone by the black tree. He lit a cigarette and took a long pull and watched the outlying land.

Playing over a thousand desperate scenarios, what John Russell must surely be enduring.

He waited.

* * *

Before the day was out Hector stumbled across the trail of the Apaches. Fresh, perhaps three hours old.

He spurred his horse. He topped out on a rise and took the mirror from his pocket and raised it overhead and angled the glass to catch the sun.

Moments later he saw the answering flash.

* * *

When Jubal rode up alone, Hector was kneeling over the tracks, rifle in hand.

"How old?" Jubal demanded.

"A few hours, not long."

"We got them." Jubal's grin stretched wide, crazed-looking below his haggard eyes. His tone verged on frantic. "We kept pushing and now we got them. I told you they'd hole up and wait out the storm."

"It was luck we found them," Hector said. He stared at Jubal's horse, its lathered coat. "Let's hope it holds out."

"Come on, let's get moving."

"Where are the men?"

"Waiting for the other scouts. They'll follow our trail and if they hear shots, they'll come running."

Hector swung up into the saddle. "Got to be careful. We're in their mountains now. If they spot us, it'll go bad for the boy."

Jubal pulled his Winchester from the scabbard. "While we've still got the light," he said and set out.

Close on their heels. Riding fast, carrying the rifles upright in the saddlebows before them.

Jubal scanned the tracks. Their mounts were still booted in rawhide, but now there was also a small herd of horses without the buckskin coverings over their iron-shod hooves. The band had met up with other Apaches driving a stolen caballada and they'd continued on together, retreating higher into the mountains.

How many gut-eaters were left in this place? Counting squaws, the Apaches outnumbered Jubal's force of a dozen men. He'd thought them only a small band, the final remnant. How many more waited at their rancheria?

They moved through the pines and he thought about Dolores and what she'd told him and the dread was heavy in his stomach like a stone.

I've seen, Papa. I've seen.

* * *

Carnoviste the chief twisted in the saddle and glanced back down the line of riders.

A lone brave came galloping past the herd of stolen horses and the warriors driving them. It was Matzus, the brave who'd pretended to take the White Eye rancher's scalp. He'd been tasked with watching their backtrail that morning, left behind to wait and observe after they'd met the other raiding party returning with their spoils of stolen horses. He shouted the alarm.

Carnoviste paused under the great pines. The captive boy sat the saddle before him, alert now, aware something was happening.

Matzus drew up at his side. "They're coming, my chief. I saw the flash of their signals."

"How far behind?" Carnoviste asked.

"If they don't spare their horses, they'll catch up with the herd before sunset."

Carnoviste was silent a long moment, trying to think, while the warriors looked on.

The medicine man stepped his horse forward. "You must act for the good of the People," Nantan said. His eyes were hidden in pine shadow. "The boy's not worth a battle. Kill him and run."

"For the good of the People the boy lives," Carnoviste said. "He brings new blood to us and restores the balance."

Nantan drew a knife. "If your hand trembles, mine is steady."

"Are you strong enough to bend my bow? The day you find that strength is the day I'll call you war chief."

"A chief needs more than sinew. He must have Power to guide him when it's time to make the hard choices."

They were all watching. Carnoviste hesitated.

"The White Eye father is coming," Nantan said. "What are you going to do?"

Carnoviste dismounted saying, "Give me the knife."

* * *

His horse smelled the blood before Jubal saw it. They were coming around a bend in the trail along the base of a low hill and the horse shied and snorted. Then Jubal spotted the carcass in the shadows ahead.

He drew up and stared.

Hector stopped beside him. "What the hell?"

The horse lay motionless in a pool of blood. Already bottleflies swarmed.

He recognized Oro despite the mutilation. Missing eyes. A strip of flesh cut away from the haunch. Next to the carcass John Russell's clothes were spread out on the pine-needles and sprinkled with blood.

Jubal rode forward.

"Hold on," Hector called. "Could be a trap." He was scanning the trees, trying to spot assassins in waiting.

Jubal got down and dropped the reins and stepped toward his son's clothes. The white shirt was wet, stained with the horse's blood. He kneeled and picked it up. A bundle in the breastpocket. He pulled it out.

It was the strip of Oro's flesh with the McKenna brand, a pair of great eyeballs wrapped inside. The horse's eyes fell out and rolled on the ground. They came to a halt staring toward some distant place beyond the pines.

Hector got down and joined him.

Jubal dropped his rifle in the dirt and kneeled looking over the slaughtered horse, the discarded clothes. What plainer warning?

"We're done," he said.

"I know."

"No farther."

"All right," Hector told him.

Jubal let out a short strangled cry. He hadn't known a man could feel so helpless.

He rose and went trudging up the hillside. When he reached the crest, he looked to the north, the knuckled ridges rising one beyond another in endless succession and the canyons between and somewhere in the sierra's vastness his son captive and lost.

After a while Hector stepped up behind him. "Not so long, then we'll come for him. We'll be back to find him."

"Too late by then," Jubal said. His face lacked all expression and he spoke like a man come to the end of things. Some ultima Thule.

"You can't believe that," Hector said.

"I don't know what to believe."

"Just a little while."

"It's not the same up here. Time runs back on itself. A little while lasts forever in this place."

"All he has to do is hold on. You too. Just hold on, all right?"

He didn't answer.

"John Russell remembers you shouted his name," Hector said. "He won't forget."

"He has to," Jubal told him. "He's got to put it out of his mind. He's got to forget everything to stay alive. To be one of them. And then when we come for him, his heart has to remember."

No sound save the wind in the pines. Slow aeolian dirge. Jubal turned and started down under the shadows.

CHAPTER FIVE

Carnoviste led them homeward. The party, now sixteen in number, descended a thousand feet along an old trail their grandfathers had made. They rode north for some time and came down another thousand feet. In such a graduation they reached the Bavispe where it was a roaring stream, rapid and girth-deep and in places deeper yet.

Carnoviste tied one end of a reata around the boy. The other end he secured about his own waist, anticipating some reckless escape, the boy committing himself to the current and the rocks. He put the horse forward into the water, his captive on the saddle behind him now.

They made the crossing and rode up onto the floodplain. Carnoviste turned the horse. The boy watched the river flowing swift and seemingly backwards to the north. Tracks of deer and turkey on the stream's alluvial fan. Somewhere the cry of an imperial woodpecker.

When the others reached them, Carnoviste set out along the floodplain and soon they came to a switchback trail at the base of a mountain. Old saddle irons and human bones lay strewn. Long ago, Mexican soldiers attempted to penetrate that high battlement. The old chieftain Juh had allowed them to climb a distance up the switchbacks before signaling his kinsmen. They'd toppled stones poised along the trail for such purpose and that night the ravens glutted.

The Apache heartland was the legacy of an ancient inferno. Volcanic palisades and parapets guarded the rancheria on the mountain, called in their tongue Pa-Gotzin-Kay, Stronghold Mountain of Paradise. Here along the borderlands of the Great Divide, the wild ones lived and hunted deer and bighorn sheep and kept the old ways. Only eagles invaded those heights.

John Russell stared down at a skull, broken and half-buried. Lurking in the empty socket a scorpion peered up at him.

* * *

A pair of boys kneeling at the edge of the cliff saw the riders approach. They watched them cross the open floodplain to draw up at the trail. The horses like ants so far below.

It was midafternoon and the warriors wouldn't reach the top until early evening. There was time for the women to prepare the feast.

One of the boys ran with the news.

* * *

Carnoviste nodded to Taza, the warrior who'd led a separate raiding party of young braves. "Lead us up the trail," he said, declining the honor of riding point.

"Are you sure, my chief?" Taza asked. "I don't deserve the glory."

"Of course you do."

"I left a brave dead in the valley. His mother and sisters will wail."

Taza's raiding party had returned with tobacco, .44 ammunition, and the small herd of horses. They'd taken their spoils without violence, but still the raiders were coming home one less than on their departure.

"No fault of yours," Carnoviste told him. "Who can guard against such accidents?"

A rabbit had startled the pony ridden by a boy on his first raid. The pony bucked him from the saddle and he fell on a rock and cracked his head and died. With few males left among the People, the loss was tragic indeed.

Taza looked at the captive White Eye boy. "My chief returns with new life," he argued, "while all I bring is fresh grief."

Carnoviste was steadfast. "The honor belongs to you."

At last Taza nodded. He stepped his mount forward and reined about to face them. "You know the price we've paid. Put on new war paint and ride proud. There's no defeat for us—we are the People."

* * *

115

After the long ride up the switchbacks, Taza led them onto the plateau. A line of boys waited to take their mounts.

Carnoviste motioned for John Russell to get down. He swung off the saddle and the chief followed suit, then two boys ran up to greet Carnoviste and he embraced his sons. Both boys were several years younger than John Russell.

The trail they'd ascended was the only way up. A natural fortress protected the rancheria. It lay on a red shelf a thousand yards wide and over two miles long, curving to the north and south, the western edge a straight plunge into a dark canyon. A steep rise of pine forest and tumbled rock shielded the eastern flank.

They started walking out across the shelf, boys leading the horses and mules.

John Russell took in the scene. Hundreds of sun-whitened cow skulls littering the ground. In the pasture a few head of cattle, horses roaming the grass. Small barren fields. The smoke of cookfires rising in thin columns. Wickiups were enshadowed on the plateau and the sun was beginning to sink behind mountain ramparts.

They followed Taza toward the village.

They'd painted their faces with fresh stripes of ochre and pounded galena, all save Carnoviste. The chief had gone to the river and washed away his faded war paint.

What they'd done in the valley below was inevitable,

Carnoviste believed. Surely it was a mistake to wish for some other way, to dream of diverging paths, for there could be no other path. Only the one set before all men, though they stride forth as fate's own executor or else linger in denial. No warrior's journey deviated so much as a footfall from that sacred course.

Even so.

It wasn't in his heart to triumph at this hour. Not over the slaughter of an unarmed woman and the besting of a courageous man. He was glad to follow behind Taza, his face scrubbed clean.

They walked in the glow of sunset and the first stars shining above and the breath of men and horses plumed in the cold twilight. At the edge of the village a woman stood waiting, a blanket about her shoulders. Her hair was long and black. Even in the distance, it struck John Russell that she was the image of Dolores. Carnoviste's eyes never strayed from her face. At her feet a dog barked, wagging its tail. Two other women stepped up beside her, plump and roundfaced and with a pair of toddlers following.

There rose from the fires a smell so sweet it made John Russell's mouth water. His stomach growled.

They greeted each other with the abrazo of their people. Braves teased younger siblings with tales of combat and theft. Fathers swung children up in their arms. The few old men who'd lived long enough to be stooped and gray looked with failing eyes on sons and grandsons and offered prayers of thanks.

Carnoviste approached Ishton, the waiting woman.

She smiled when he brushed her hair back. Neither of them spoke. He rested his arm across her shoulders and they stood with his other wives while the little ones hugged his legs.

A worried-looking woman scanned the faces of the braves, her daughter of perhaps thirteen winters and another much smaller girl at her side. When Taza stepped toward them, the older girl gripped her mother's hand.

"My sister," Taza said. "I bring you bad news. Meet this thing with strength as your son would want you to do."

The woman shrieked. John Russell saw her take a knife from the fold of her moccasin. She tore her muslin blouse and cut her breasts and arms, sobbing, groaning, and she reached behind her neck and took the long braid of hair that fell to her knees and she cut it. She threw the braid down. Her young daughters watched, then erupted into their own wailing grief.

* * *

Singers and drummers gathered about the central fire. Carnoviste, dressed now in his finery, led the warriors to their places. He sat down on a blanket and motioned for an old man to take a seat of honor at his left. Nantan, the shaman, sat at his right. The other warriors formed a semicircle around the fire while women and children sat behind the men.

John Russell lowered himself beside the chief's sons. One of them pointed at John Russell's pale skin and said something to his brother. They laughed.

He ignored them, looking for the mourning girls and the woman who'd cut herself, but they weren't there.

The Apaches were greater in number than he'd have guessed from the rumors told in the valley. He'd always thought them just a few small scattered bands. Dolores had never liked to speak of specifics. Gathered now in their stronghold they were more than the lowlanders supposed. The boy counted perhaps twenty warriors with many other youths approaching fighting age.

Carnoviste raised his hand. Everyone fell silent.

He rolled tobacco in an oak leaf. He took a bright gleed from the fire with his naked hand and lit the cigarette and dropped the coal into the flames. Then he blew smoke in the four cardinal directions and raised his arm. The women rose and began serving food.

There was venison and honey and meal cakes made of the sweet acorns that were piled everywhere in the village. The women had prepared jugs of tiswin, but first they filled the men's cups with mescal. No one started eating until all the warriors had been served, then the chief raised his cup and they ate. Women saw to the filling of dishes for themselves and the children.

Two of the chief's wives handed plates to their sons,

then sat holding steaming bowls. Toddlers came and sat in their laps and the women opened their shirts to let them nurse while they ate.

Hunger was sharp in John Russell's belly. Dogs huddled begging scraps and he gave some thought to joining them.

Then she was standing over him in her beaded buckskin robes. He looked up at the woman he felt sure was Dolores's older sister. Ishton smiled and gave him a warm bowl, then took her seat behind Carnoviste.

He ate. Nothing ever tasted so wonderful. He didn't care that the meat was undercooked and bloody. He gripped it with his fingers and took great bites, grease and blood running down his arms, dripping from his chin.

When he heard the wails, he stopped chewing. They all listened, the woman's cries of grief rising on the wind, falling away in darkness.

Carnoviste rose. He spoke the name of the dead boy, afterward to go unvoiced for fear of summoning his ghost. "He showed courage on his first raid," the chief said. "He waits for us in the Other World where the game is always fat and plenty and the grass green. His mother and sisters will be cared for."

John Russell didn't understand a word of what was said. The boy ate the last of his meal and studied his captors in the firelight.

"Now we celebrate the return of our warriors," Carnoviste told them.

The drummers faced east. They began beating out a driving rhythm on their goatskin drums with sliding blows from sticks with rounded ends. A breeze spirited up sparks from the fire and they swirled among the stars.

John Russell saw the brave who'd shown him the bloody scalp rise before the fire. Later he'd learn the brave's name, Matzus, and his hatred for him and the old hag would burn on forever. Matzus overturned his cup of mescal, spilling the remnants on the ground. Libation to the dead. He crouched and stalked slowly forward until he stood motionless in front of a group of children. No sound save the beat of the drums. Matzus raised his eyes to meet their own. Then he jumped at the children, making a stabbing motion, and they cried out in peals of laughter.

He spun on his heel and called to his wife. She went and got his pistol and handed it to him. Matzus raised the revolver and danced about the fire four times and stopped. He sang his exploits. Other braves rose, clowning or acting out feats of courage.

Everyone stood up to join in the singing. One man got out his crude fiddle, the sound box constructed from a yucca stalk and painted with designs of lightning bolts and mountains. A string of sinew was tied to the tuning peg.

The boy watched them go clockwise about the fire, improvising steps, parodying old battles. He could feel the pulse of the drums and dancing feet in the ground. Carnoviste danced. The tribal musicians played before their chief on fiddle and bone-flute and drums while dancers wheeled about the blaze.

Then his captors required of him a song.

When they completed the fourth circle, Carnoviste stepped out and grabbed the boy. He chanted several low notes and jabbed a finger at John Russell's mouth.

John Russell shook his head. The drums were throbbing.

Carnoviste clapped him hard on the back, shoving him into the firelight.

The boy started belting out *Old Dan Tucker*, the first song that came to him. They watched him dance a desperate little jig.

He finished and the Apaches whooped, demanding more. He sang *Barbara Allen*, but the sad melody wasn't to their liking so he switched back to *Dan Tucker* and hopped about.

After a while they grew bored of him. To his relief John Russell was allowed to sit back down.

The medicine man started chanting. Horns jutted from his buffalo cap nightmarish and weird in the shadows. He sang his prayer and turned rapidly, touching the heel of his crippled foot to the ground, shaking a deerhoof rattle. His chant rose to a high pitch. The drumbeats coming faster now, the hands of the drummers blazing, and then the widows came out to dance.

Mothers sent young children off to bed.

The widows brushed their hair back, making certain the men were watching. The tribe had provided for their well-being, but the appropriate time of mourning was at an end and tonight the People's strict morals would be relaxed for them to earn their livelihood in the dance. None would remain widows much longer. A lone divorcée with a cut-nose joined them.

The wives said nothing. All must eat, even cut-nosed harlots. In the morning order would return and whoever transgressed thereafter must face harsh punishment.

But tonight they danced.

The mothers of Carnoviste's sons escorted their children away, leading them to the separate wickiups that had been built for each wife. When the young ones were inside, the mothers returned and sat stoic.

The widows tore off their blouses. Breasts rose and fell. Hips swaying, legs flashing under skirts. Their hair was still short from when they'd cut it in mourning and some were marked with the scars of healed cuts, visible memories of grief.

Zunde, the big warrior who'd knocked John Russell down in the ambush, sat drinking tiswin. He saw Taza and the other raiders join the dance. Zunde called to his old friend, but the warrior ignored him.

Taza was dancing with a girl who'd been widowed since the summer. He held a bottle of mescal and placed his other hand on her hip and she leaned in and whispered what she wanted, a horse, blankets, the feather pillow he'd carried back with him.

He protested the pillow, a gift for his wife. The girl slipped from his grasp and danced with one of the young braves. Taza frowned. Zunde spewed tiswin and laughed.

Taza grabbed her arm and spun her to face him. "The pillow is yours," he said. She jerked her arm free and turned and walked off into the dark. Taza followed, sipping from the bottle.

Deals were struck, bargains made. John Russell saw Matzus dancing with a plump widow and the cut-nose woman, slowly making his choice, then moving in close against the widow as the harlot's eyes flashed. Matzus and the widow left the others to their dance.

Carnoviste took Ishton's hand and they rose. The boy watched her, firelight on raven hair as the chief walked with her to their wickiup.

The night air was cold. John Russell looked amid the vast heavens where constellations spun about the polestar and under their cold and distant light it was then he wept.

He felt a hand grip his ear, twisting hard. He rose under the grasp of Carnoviste's plumpest wife. She spoke in Apache and gestured toward a wickiup, where her boy was peeking out the flap of hide, and made him understand he was to join them.

John Russell wiped away his tears and slowly

followed his captor's wife into the wickiup.

* * *

Carnoviste and Ishton lay together on a bed of hides. A small fire burned in the wickiup and shone on Ishton's copper body.

His other wives had given him sons, but Ishton remained barren as a stone. The women whispered it was because she'd stared at an owl when she was a girl. It didn't matter to him. She was always the first he'd choose to spend the night beside, the only one who understood his fears for the People's future and the burden he shouldered.

"The boy's strong," Carnoviste told her. "Almost cracked my head with a rock."

"He tries to kill you and you feel pride?"

"I'm glad he's not a coward. Someday his courage will serve the People."

"You still believe it had to be this way?" she asked.

"There was no choice. The balance of blood had to be set right. Even though it will make things hard for a while. This won't be an easy winter—we can't risk going down to the foothills now."

"Some warriors think it would still be worth the danger to winter below."

"They're wrong. If the White Eye catches us below, he'll slaughter everyone now."

"We'll be all right up here," she said. "You didn't start this. The People know it's not your fault and they follow your counsel."

"Nantan's counsel is louder than mine."

"An old man who limps."

"He limps, but his Power is strong. I've seen bullets pass through him without harm. Sometimes I think his Power has led him down the Path of Darkness. Nantan agreed it was our duty to take the boy, but when the White Eye chased us, he wanted to cut his throat and run."

She crooked her elbow, resting her head on her palm, and lay looking at him. "Will they stop searching for him?"

"It doesn't matter. They'll never find him." There was a pause. Then he asked, "Do you miss her?"

"She was my little sister. Of course I do."

Neither of them would speak her name, the lost girl counted among the dead.

"Gouyen still weeps for her," Ishton told him. "She was like a granddaughter to her. It almost killed the old woman to send her away."

"Now she's had revenge to satisfy her."

"I doubt it's enough to ease her grief. It brings no comfort to me."

She stared into the fire. Eyes soft with sorrow.

"I'm sorry," he said.

"For what?"

"Making you remember."

"Don't be sorry," she told him.

She leaned in close and her hair rained over him and he could smell the fragrant suds with which she'd washed, the pounded roots of the amole, and the night went on slow and sweet.

* * *

John Russell woke at dawn, the chief's wife giving his ribs a kick as she stepped over him and out the wickiup. He grunted and lay holding himself. The chief's son hopped over and pushed away the hide flap covering the opening.

John Russell could hear them singing outside.

Carnoviste stood facing the rising sun. He sang the Morning Song, his face and arms raised to Ussen, and thanked the Creator of Life for the love between man and woman, a holy thing, and welcomed the new day.

Then he gathered up the captive and a group of boys including his sons Neiflint and Oblite, half-brothers who'd yet to see their tenth winter. He led them out across the plain to where the ground rose and a little stream ran in the woods. The boys trudged ill-tempered and complaining. Carnoviste cut a switch along the way and they quieted.

They stood over the pool where the spring emptied. Ice on the water. He motioned to the captive boy and his sons. "Break it," he said. "The rest of you get a fire started."

Neiflint and Oblite attacked the ice with rocks. John Russell couldn't understand the chief's orders, but he followed the brothers' lead.

The others set about building a fire on the banks, piling dry brush and branches. One boy got out his firestick and went to work. Soon he had a flame going in the kindling and the boys kneeled coaxing it.

When it was burning strong, Carnoviste told them, "Line up and strip."

They stood naked in a row.

"Jump," Carnoviste ordered.

At his command all the boys save the captive jumped into the cold pool.

John Russell's buckskins lay in a pile at his feet. He looked at Carnoviste and he looked at the boys who burst up from the water roaring their lungs out. They staggered onto the bank.

Carnoviste barked at him in Apache and the switch stung his backside. John Russell jumped. He splashed into the pool, the cold shocking him, engulfed in an icy embrace, then he rose naked and trembling. He screamed like a child born of the water.

He climbed up the bank, teeth chattering, arms tight around himself, and huddled with the boys about the fire. They took deep belly-breaths and the cold made them feel vital, alive. Carnoviste let them warm themselves a while.

"What does this teach you?" he asked.

"To be strong," Neiflint said.

"Not to be afraid when it hurts," Oblite said.

"Someday you'll be courageous warriors," Carnoviste told them. "Because you've made yourself stronger than pain. Now jump again."

The boys groaned.

* * *

Over the next days he was watched closely in the village, never allowed to go anywhere unaccompanied. He slept at the opening of the wickiup. Every morning he rose to the greeting of the woman's foot in his side.

She was Oblite's mother and her plump face bore a constant impassive expression. She gave him the chore of collecting firewood. While he gathered branches in the pines, she stood watching, a baby strapped to her back. He carried the heavy loads in his arms and whenever she thought him slow or clumsy, she'd smack his head with a stick.

She only spoke to issue inscrutable orders or berate him for some dereliction. In her eyes he was an article of plunder, not fully human.

John Russell noticed she never struck him in sight of her husband. When Carnoviste was nearby, the boy was accorded some degree of dignity.

In the evenings behind the hide walls of the wickiup he was tasked with picking lice from her hair and Oblite's hair. One by one he'd get them between his fingers and flick the things into the fire. They burst in the flames, a soft popping sound.

At first the job disgusted him. He imagined thousands of the little creatures crawling over his body. Then it wasn't long before his scalp was infested as well and he saw to his own grooming.

* * *

One afternoon he was carrying a load of firewood when Carnoviste shouted at several boys and girls playing the hoop and pole game. They abandoned the game and took off running across the plateau. Carnoviste looked at John Russell. He gestured toward the timbered hill where they were headed, back the way the boy had just come. John Russell began to set the load down.

Carnoviste shook his head. "Get moving," he told the boy.

He ran. The others were also lugging burdens, large rocks they'd paused to pick up, knowing it was expected of them. By the time he neared the crest they'd already turned and started racing back. They made faces at him when they passed. At the top of the hill he was breathing hard, but he hadn't dropped the firewood.

He stood in the pine shadows looking out over the

plateau and the wickiups, the peaks that rose beyond the river. It was the first time he'd had a moment to himself since the night they'd arrived at the stronghold. A sense of longing overcame him, deep and bitter. As though the heart inside him was dying.

In that moment he resolved to either escape or force the Apaches to kill him.

* * *

The wickiups all faced east. They were insulated with animal hides and banked with soil taken from the firepits. The chief's wickiups stood in the center of the village, one for each of his wives.

While the woman, the baby, and Oblite were sleeping, John Russell lay awake in his place by the flap. He watched the smoke from the fire rising up through the hole in the hides and he thought about his predicament.

Many of the warriors' wives looked Mexican, not Apache. He wondered if they'd all been taken from their families as children, or if out of madness or desperation some had chosen this life.

In the rancheria there was a Mexican boy about John Russell's age. Like him a prisoner and slave. He was under the charge of the medicine man Nantan. John Russell bided his time and watched for a chance to approach. If only they might engineer a moment alone, he was certain he'd discover the boy also plotted escape,

131

certain to find a fellow strategist.

Apache boys had no responsibilities save the day's training. Their parents indulged them at every turn. They spent their time hunting and playing and riding in the pasture while John Russell fulfilled the squaw's every whim. He was a pariah among the other children. For the time being, Carnoviste had no use for him save that he should train with the others.

Only Ishton, his captor's favored wife, treated him with kindness. She saw to it that he ate well. She was perhaps only four years older than himself and from time to time she'd borrow him from his mistress with the excuse of some chore, but in truth he was free to rest or walk the woods with her. He often wished the other boy had such a friend in his trouble.

Then came the evening he was sent to fill waterjugs. When John Russell approached the spring, he saw the Mexican boy kneeling at the pool. There were tears in his eyes. He heard John Russell coming and quickly wiped them away and rose lifting a clay olla.

He called to the boy in Spanish. "Wait, don't go. I'm John Russell McKenna. What's your name?"

The boy looked at him. He opened his mouth as though to speak, then scowled in frustration and shook his head. He marched past him on the trail.

"Hold on. It's all right if you can't remember."

He ran up and touched the boy's shoulder. The boy spun around and dropped the olla and hit John Russell in the face. The olla shattered at their feet, water spilling. The boy yelled in Apache. He bent and picked up a shard of clay and threw it.

John Russell dodged the shard. "I'm trying to help you," he said.

The boy turned and started walking empty-handed back toward the village. John Russell stood at the spring watching him go.

He never felt more alone.

CHAPTER SIX

Griffin, Pennsylvania

December, 1928

Day four of the Python Coal strike. Outside the company gates, striking miners sang Joe Hill songs and blocked off the road. They raised signs painted with union slogans. Wives and children stood beside men with callused hands and weary eyes.

The operative for the Continental Detective Agency stood in the mine yard, Stetson cocked on his head, billy club dangling from his right hand. His name was Cain. His hair, once raven black, was now shot through with silver. Those eyes were given to darkness, so deep-set were they above sharp cheekbones that lent his smooth face a taut and predatory appearance. A column of enforcers stood behind him, off-duty deputies augmenting his squad of detectives.

Strikers belted out the chorus to *The Preacher and*

the Slave.

Detectives gripped hoses and lengths of lead pipe.

Rain started falling in the dawnlight. The breaker plant loomed nine stories above them, the hulking asymmetrical façade of a silent fortress, its massive crushers no longer thundering.

Griffin was a company town through and through. The inflated company scrip, worthless fiat, was accepted only at company stores. Miners racked up debt. Miners toiled in danger, suffered black lung and broken bodies. Python awarded bonuses to executives who honored company priorities—keep production costs low.

Workers pleaded to be heard. Python tightened its hold.

The workers staged a walk-out demanding better pay and shorter hours. They went red. They joined the IWW. Company bosses fired the Wobblies and evicted them from Python-owned housing while the strike raged on. Governor Prentiss, a Python shareholder, threatened to send in the National Guard if miners persisted in displays of Bolshevik fervor. Rumors circulated among the Wobblies that Mother Jones, the most dangerous woman in America, would soon arrive to rally her brood.

"You got the time, Mo?" Cain asked.

A tall negro stepped up beside him and opened his pocketwatch. "Quarter after seven, Sergeant," Mosby said. "Trucks ought to be here any second."

"They're late. I wisht I'd sent more guards to ride

with em."

"Be along directly, I expect."

Side by side they were a study in contrast. Cain short and barrel-chested, the much-younger negro almost a foot taller and lanky. Twelve years earlier they'd met during the Punitive Expedition, riding with Black Jack Pershing to chase Pancho Villa deep into Mexico. At the time Cain was an ex-sergeant in the 4th Cavalry turned civilian scout, Mosby a green recruit in the negro 10th. They'd been serving together ever since.

Mosby took off his steel-rimmed glasses. He wiped raindrops from the lenses with a handkerchief.

"Hey, coon," a ragged voice called from beyond the chainlink fence. "You a Continental coon? They'll hire anybody, won't they?"

Mosby ignored the taunt.

Cain glanced over. The striker looked decades older than he likely was, stooped from shoveling in the low-ceilinged tunnels ten hours a day. He was waving his middle finger.

"I never seen a Continental coon before."

A hacking cough shook the man's thin frame. He leaned on the fence fighting for breath. "You skull crackin son of a bitch," he choked out.

Mosby put his glasses back on and ignored him.

Rain streamed down Cain's slicker. He heard the trucks coming, heading up the road toward the mine, and steeled himself for the arrival. He raised his hat and rubbed his right temple. He could feel one of the headaches coming on and he didn't need to deal with that, not now, not with the trucks on the way.

The striker with the bad lungs started in once more. "What they payin you to beat down honest folks? We got little kids liable to starve, their daddies can't afford to feed em."

Mosby wasn't listening, focused instead on Cain's orders.

"Gas masks on," Cain shouted. "Get ready to open that gate."

Cain took off his Stetson. He donned his own gas mask and tightened the strap, then put his hat back on loosely. A dull ache behind his right temple. He ignored it, a man with a job to do.

The masked enforcers looked like giant bipedal bugs. They readied tear gas grenades.

The first truck hove into sight, a scab crew in the bed. Company bosses shipped in European strike-breakers, immigrants from northern Italy, offering them wages lower than those the miners had walked out over. The scabs were happy to get it.

Python paid off congressmen to back favorable immigration policies. Immigrants were surplus pools of cheap labor. For American workers struggling to survive, they meant wage deflation, loss of job security. Company bosses opened their arms wide, did the New Colossus bit: Give me your poor, your huddled masses.

The strikers were coughing, cursing, but still they refused to fall back.

The rock that hit Mosby came out of nowhere. It thudded into the side of his head and he staggered forward, dazed. Cain jerked him out of the truck's path as it went rumbling by.

"You all right, Mo?"

He groaned. Blood ran down his scalp.

Cain spotted the miner who'd been running his mouth at Mosby earlier. The stooped man was hurrying from the gate, fleeing into the crowd.

Cain motioned to a big deputy. "Get Mosby into the office."

The deputy took him, Mosby draping an arm across his shoulders, and they hobbled toward the mine office.

Cain grabbed two detectives. "Follow me," he ordered. They marched out the gate and waded into the strikers, Cain swinging his billy club, making a path.

When he caught up with the stooped miner, Cain spun the man around to face him. His eyes went wide. Cain slammed the billy club into his face and heard the man's nose crunch.

The last truck passed through the gate.

Cain reared back and came down hard. Blood and teeth went flying. The striker dropped to his knees and Cain grabbed a fistful of hair and jerked his head up. The striker's teeth had torn through his lower lip.

The pair of detectives were holding off enraged miners, their pipes sweeping the air, giving Cain room to work. He swung the billy club and broke the man's jaw.

A striker rushed in and tried to throw a sucker punch at Cain, but one of the Continentals dropped him before the blow could land.

Cain let his man fall in the mud. He lay motionless, bleeding out his ears, breath coming slow and pained. Cain kicked him in the ribs and turned back to the gate.

He looked for the two detectives to make sure they were following, saw them deep in the crowd, strikers ganging up. A detective went down. Miners on all sides started kicking and stomping.

The other Continental op turned to help his partner— then a striker swung a 2x4 against his back and the detective dropped to his knees.

Cain was pushing his way toward his fallen detectives when he heard the roar of full-auto gunfire. He looked back over his shoulder and cursed—

Muzzle flash in the mine tipple.

Bullets cut down strikers. Bullets tore through protest signs.

An old lady fell with half a dozen holes in her torso. A man's face exploded. Women screamed. Blood misted from a boy's kneecap and he hit the ground, panic on his face, and tried to crawl through the mud, but running feet trampled over him.

The crowd rushed for their cars parked along the ditch.

Cain ran back through the gate waving his arms up at the tipple. Detectives and deputies looked on in confusion, unsure what to do, their world rendered half-unreal.

Cain threw down the billy club and tore his mask off. He snatched a Lee-Enfield from a deputy's arms and raised the rifle to his shoulder and worked the bolt. He drew a bead.

Edgewater was still firing from his perch in the tipple, mowing down the strikers.

Cain squeezed the trigger.

The bullet burst through the machine gunner's skull and everything went quiet.

Cain lowered the rifle. He turned and stared out the gate.

From where he stood he counted nine for sure dead. Three women, six men. Several wounded were trying to hide in the weeds along the ditch. Cars sped down the road, racing to the hospital in town or the tent camp where the strikers lived.

"Damn it all to hell," Cain said.

* * *

They sent a Rolls-Royce Phantom for Cain. When he slid inside, the backseat smelled of pipesmoke and almonds.

The chauffer drove him twenty miles to Carbondale and the country club named Elysian Fields.

He met the Python executive on the patio overlooking the golf course. It was a cold December day and they had the patio all to themselves, no one else about. The man wore a white suit and gold cufflinks under his heavy topcoat. Cain's trenchcoat was bloodstained, his boots covered in dried mud.

While Cain briefed him on the morning's massacre, the boss smoked a cigar and drank cognac from a snifter—local cops turned a blind eye to Elysian Fields' private bar. The Volstead Act went unenforced on club grounds.

"My damn fault," Cain said. "I put that shell-shocked boy up in the tipple. He still had a screw loose from his time over there. Comin home without a face. I reckon he seen them clouds of gas risin up down below, saw our boys get taken by the mob, and somethin in him just snapped."

"You were hired to suppress a strike," the boss said. "Not create martyrs."

"What do you want me to do?"

"Maybe you were mistaken about the sequence of events. The papers can set it right for public edification. Your war hero died first. A red sniper killed the brave young lad and only after that tragedy did your men fire on armed hostiles. I want it made clear the majority of worker casualties were the result of friendly fire by their own ranks."

"You can get the papers to run with that?"

"Those owned by subsidiaries of our holding company."

"And the others?"

"The Wobblies will have their martyrs. A few dead bodies are like an answered prayer for them. Spilt milk to make their point. But they're going to have one more body than they realize."

The boss looked at him.

"What are you tryin to tell me?" Cain asked.

"They want martyrs, why stop here? Give them a real martyr. If we're forced to weather this shitstorm you caused, then we make it count for more than a handful of dead miners. Cut the head off the snake."

The boss glanced around. The patio remained empty.

"The Wobblies are holding a rally tonight. Brubeck's leading it. He says they're not going to back down after today."

Michael Brubeck was an IWW organizer, a man committed body and soul to the cause of the union.

"He's a fiery personality," the boss said. "Which hasn't always served him well. He has a well-known tendency of making enemies within his own organization."

Cain stared, not saying a word. He waited for it.

"Try to make it look internecine. A former comrade with a personal grievance."

"A massacre ain't enough for you?" Cain asked.

The boss sipped cognac. He offered Cain five grand for the hit.

"Go to hell," Cain told him.

"Six cold," the boss said. "Final offer."

"It wasn't a negotiation tactic. I meant go to hell."

"Plenty of other guys willing to work for a living," the boss said. "More competitive rates too. I thought you might want a chance at redemption."

"I'd rather be damned," Cain said and rose from the table.

* * *

That evening he sat on the bed in his room at the boarding house, his boots off, holes in his socks. He took a pull from a bottle of Canadian whiskey.

Light from the streetlamps bled through lace curtains. Dim noises on the street outside. Passing cars, a dog barking.

The room was spartan, the way he liked it—one suitcase on the dresser, never unpacked. His .45 on the nightstand, shotgun propped against the desk. Tools of the trade.

He massaged his right hand. A deep ache there. The knuckles flattened, marked with pale keloid starbursts.

He couldn't stop thinking about Edgewater, his hideous grin, what Cain would have to write the boy's mother in Memphis. Dear Madam, I regret to inform you...

A newspaper rested on the nightstand, that morning's edition, old news of a world with one less massacre than it now contained this evening, and he opened it looking for something to keep his mind busy.

He read the paper and sipped whiskey, waiting on Mosby to come by so he could tell him their own news. They were free agents again. After he'd finished with the Python exec, he'd phoned the old man at Continental headquarters and told him where to go as well.

On page three he came to a story that stopped him cold. It was only a few paragraphs long, sandwiched between a piece on Dow Jones losses and a review of Buster Keaton's latest. He put the bottle away. When he'd come to the end of the article, he started reading it over.

By the time the knock sounded at his door Cain had read it four times.

"Who is it?" he called.

"It's me, Sergeant," Mosby said.

"Hold on."

Cain got up and crossed the room and unlocked the door. He pulled it wide.

Mosby stood in the hall, cap in hand.

"Come on in," Cain told him. "How's your noggin, Mo?"

The doctor had shaved his head to stitch the gash.

Mosby stepped inside and ran his palm over his bald dome. "You know me, Sergeant. Got a head harder than a rock."

"I wisht you'd figure out you don't have to call me that no more."

"Reckon you're right, sir. We ain't neither of us soldiers no more, bustin skulls for the company."

"Set down. You want a smoke?"

"I believe I'll pass." He sat in the desk chair. "What's the news you got for me?"

Cain took a pack of Camels from the nightstand. He slipped a matchbook from his pocket and struck a match on the striker pad and got the cigarette burning.

"Boss man offered me a little side work."

"Is that right?" Mosby said, looking away. "Well, money hard to come by. Can't fault you none for takin what comes along."

"You goin to ask what the job was?"

"I reckon somethin to do with that Brubeck fella holdin the rally across town. Not the kind of work I'd want to be part of. You don't mind me sayin, sir."

"You reckon right. He offered me six cash to kill Brubeck."

Mosby didn't speak.

Cain took a long drag. "You know what I told him?"

"No, sir."

"I said I'm a soldier, not a damn button man."

Mosby grinned in relief. "I'm glad to hear you say

that. Tell you the truth, I got a bone to pick with this outfit."

"We're done with the agency. Never again."

"You ain't turned red on me, now have you, Sergeant?"

"I ain't turned red. Just done crackin skulls for rich sons of bitches."

Mosby became serious. "What happened this mornin, Sergeant? How the hell did somethin like that cut loose?"

"Nothin but a damned massacre."

"Ain't like it used to be. Least not the way I remember things. Maybe I'm just gettin old."

Mosby was thirty, trim and fit. Cain a solid fifty-eight.

"You're still a young buck," Cain said. "I'm the one that's old. Pretty soon I'll be useless."

"Come on now, Sergeant. That ain't true. Man like you never gonna be useless. You'll always have plenty to teach folks."

"You don't want to know the things I've learned. Can't teach it to nobody anyhow. Except to say it ain't worth a damn."

"Why you want to talk that way, Sergeant? You can still out-do fellas half your age."

"You remember old R. C. Slater rode with us in Chihuahua?"

Mosby nodded. "Fine scout. Almost as good as you and the Apaches we had with us."

"R. C.'s maybe ten years older than me. At the most.

His kids put him in a home in Denver. I went to see him when I was out there last summer. When I come in, he didn't even get out of bed, too weak and shriveled up. We got to talkin and it was plain he still had all his marbles, his body was just fallin apart. After a while this nurse comes in, pretty young thing, and she says, It's time to go pee pee."

He made a gesture with the cigarette. "This is a grown man she's talkin to. Killed enemies in three foreign countries, rode thousands of miles chasin Pancho, screwed the fattest whores in Chihuahua, and she tells him it's time to go pee pee."

"You say she was good lookin, though? I bet old R. C. enjoyed havin her tend to him."

"Well, that ain't the end of it. She finally gets him up out of bed and they shuffle across this little room he's in and they go in the can together. She leaves the door open a crack and I can see in the mirror she's aimin his pecker for him. R. C. just stands there hunched over and does his business while she's holdin it."

Mosby shook his head slowly.

"Point bein," Cain said, "if they told you that someday you'd have a pretty girl hold your pecker ever time you took a piss, well, it might sound a whole lot different than it actually is."

"There's worse places to end up," Mosby told him. "You and me seen some of em."

"I'm tired, Mo. Tired of the jobs, tired of it all. I

want to be a soldier again. You remember what it was to be a soldier?"

"Yessir. Even campin out in the desert, eatin Pancho's dust was better than this."

Cain stepped to the window and pushed the curtain aside. Headlights moving on the street below, the shining marquee of the Aztec Theatre. *The Wind* and *The Man Who Laughs* were playing tonight.

It was his practice never to open curtains, never linger in front of a window. The code kept him alive. Where he was standing now a sniper could take him out with one shot.

Let them try. It wasn't his fate to die here. He knew it in his blood—nothing could destroy him now, no force on earth, until he set foot in that final country.

"You ever heard of the Sierra Madre?" Cain asked. "A mountain range in Old Mexico, some of the roughest country in the world. I was there once when I was just a kid. I saw Geronimo surrender."

"You seen Geronimo hisself? I didn't know that about you, Sergeant. But what's them mountains got to do with us?"

Cain sat back on the bed and tossed the newspaper to Mosby. "Apaches murdered a rancher's wife and kidnapped his son, took the boy up into the sierras."

"Same kind of Apaches that scouted for us, huntin Pancho?"

"Those were half-tame Apaches. These are broncos,

never got shipped to a reservation."

The article quoted a paper out of Arizona, *The Douglas Daily Dispatch*, relaying word of the ambush on the rancher's family, how the savages slaughtered Mrs. McKenna, then with "blood-curdling war whoops" carried off the boy, "doubtlessly condemned to a life of barbarism in the redman's last accursed bastion." The journalist was no Richard Harding Davis, but he knew how to paint a picture, Cain would give him that. The article noted that the boy was an epileptic and his father was deeply concerned for his health.

"Wild Indins," Mosby said, looking over the paper. "In this day and age. Well, son of a buck."

"Don't you see it, Mo? This is our chance to be soldiers again. My last chance."

"You gonna fight a Indin war? Ain't it a little late for that?"

"Let's be what we are," Cain told him. "One more time. You with me, Mo?"

"Sergeant, I reckon you know I'd follow you anywheres."

"Good man, Mosby." He rose to shake his hand, then abruptly sank back down again, grimacing.

"You all right?"

"Just a damned headache. Ain't nothin."

"You best get some rest after a day from hell like this one."

"I reckon so."

152

Mosby rose and stepped to the door. "I'll see you in the mornin, Sergeant."

* * *

When Mosby was gone, Cain closed his eyes and pressed his palms to his temples and squeezed. The headache he'd managed to suppress that morning was fast returning. He opened his eyes and the room swam before him, rocking like a ship on rough seas. He saw a creeping blackness at the corner of his vision and wherever he turned his head the darkness was present and spreading farther.

It wasn't the first time his vision had presaged one of the headaches. Cain fought its coming the only way he knew how.

He went to his suitcase and opened it and took out the kalis. The blade was double-edged, sheathed in a narra wood scabbard lashed with rattan bindings. He unsheathed it and held it upright. A naga or serpent head was carved at the base. The blade curved in three waves before straightening at the point so that the weapon mimicked a slithering viper.

Decades earlier he'd taken it off the body of a Moro warrior in the Philippines.

In the country of its origin the kalis had been passed father to son for six generations, the chain broken by a stranger to that archipelago where he himself had seen the only true father he'd ever known cut down.

He called the kalis Wormwood. It had crossed oceans with him in the intervening years, drawn the blood of alien races, and been washed clean in rivers whose names appeared on no atlas anywhere.

Cain locked the door and drew the curtains. He switched off the lights, then lowered himself to the floor and crossed his legs, placing a foot on either thigh, and gripped the kalis with both hands, elbows extended. Closing his eyes he began to meditate as he'd learned long ago on the island of Bali. In those days meditation had kept his mind from the secret he carried, the old confession following him like a shadow that reached all the way to hell.

He conjured a darkness. Then he imagined a blue dot at the center of that nothingness and he concentrated on the dot until the world around him faded. He peered into the dot. A blackness deeper yet. At its core a succession of rings and dots, a place he called the Zero. His awareness drew inward upon himself. He passed through the infinite rings, going down into the Zero, staying always one step ahead of the shadow that pursued his waking mind.

When the full-force of the headache came, he was too deep within the Zero for the pain to register.

* * *

Late that night four masked men burst into the home of Michael Brubeck. They pistol-whipped the union organizer in front of his young wife and children before dragging him outside and shoving him into an idling Model A.

The kidnappers gagged Brubeck and tied his hands and feet. He lay in the floorboard on the long drive out to the ghost town.

The mines in that area were long abandoned. A coal seam hundreds of feet below ground had spontaneously ignited decades earlier and the underground inferno forced Python to close the entire town.

The Ford went slowly up Main Street. The road broken and cracked, windows into hell. At its heart the blaze was hotter than the surface of the planet Mercury and it would be burning there for another century to come. Trees wilted from the tongues of heat snapping at their roots. Sinkholes were known to open in overgrown front lawns, plumes of steam billowing from the void. Sulfurous, reeking.

"Welcome to Helltown," one of the kidnappers said.

The next morning a sheriff's deputy got the anonymous tip and drove out to the ghost town. He found Brubeck hanging from a dead tree in the town square, IWW scrawled in coal dust across his forehead.

CHAPTER SEVEN

When John Russell was sure no one was watching, he slipped into the empty wickiup. An old saddle lay against the wall, a rope hackamore draped across the pommel. He raised his buckskin shirt and took the hackamore and coiled it about his waist, then let his shirt fall covering the rope.

He stepped back outside into the afternoon light. His mistress Tsaltey-koo sat nearby, sewing a pair of leggings. He sat down within sight of her and made a show of loafing, stretching out and staring up at the clouds.

The last few times she'd sent him for firewood she remained in the village, the captive boy trusted enough to go alone. Their supply was getting low now and his plan counted on her sending him again today.

Tsaltey-koo frowned. She got to her feet and came over and kicked his leg. She spoke in harsh Apache and pointed to the woods.

The boy sighed and rose.

He started walking out across the plateau toward the

rise of pines. When he'd gone some distance from the village, he changed course, heading for the switchback trail that led down the mountain.

John Russell approached a mule grazing in the pasture. He uncoiled the rope and got the hackamore on the mule.

A trail guard was posted in a stand of rocks at the cliff's edge. The switchbacks were always watched, a duty shared in alternating shifts by all those in the village who were of age. He'd thought about trying to kill the guard, whoever it might be, even if a squaw stood watch, but there was no way of getting close, impossible to sneak up on an Apache. He'd just have to make a run for it. The most he could hope for was a lead. It would take the guard time to run back and alert the warriors, time for them to mount up and start after him. In his desperation he believed it was enough.

John Russell swung up on the mule bareback. He took the trail and started down the mountain, riding at a rapid clip, then there was a shout from the unseen guard. He kept going and didn't look back.

At his side a steep plunge, broken rocks far below.

"Don't fall," he told the mule.

By the time he heard their hoofbeats above him, coming fast, he was still a long way from the bottom. He sped around a bend without care or caution and gave the mule his heels and kept the lead down the switchbacks. When he reached the foot of the trail, his pursuers were gaining on him.

John Russell crossed the river and rode along the banks at the edge of the woods. A pine branch hung low. He stopped the mule and glanced back to make sure his pursuers hadn't spotted him. Then he grabbed the limb and kicked his mount in the ribs and swung up into the tree, the mule running on down the floodplain and out of sight.

The Apaches were coming. He climbed across the bough and dropped into the undergrowth. A woodpecker hammered somewhere ahead. John Russell raced deep into the woods.

* * *

Carnoviste rode up onto the banks ahead of Zunde and Pericho. They followed the mule's tracks down the floodplain. They'd gone some distance when Carnoviste noticed the hoofprints were wrong, too shallow in the sand.

He reined his mule and drew up.

"We missed it," he told the warriors. "He abandoned the mule."

He turned and went back. Soon he found the place where the tracks ran under the pine branch. He dismounted and called for the others to stake the mounts, then he left his mule standing there and darted into the pines.

The hammering of a woodpecker echoed. Carnoviste moved through the woods, scanning the ground for sign, bent undergrowth or bruised lichen, and he fingered the medicine bag hanging from his neck.

A rush came over him. The flood of a Power he didn't command. It flowed through him, driving him on. He couldn't say how he knew, but he was certain the boy was in great danger and there was little time left.

Carnoviste found his tracks and followed at a run, no need to hesitate or second guess. The Power guiding him was strong. He could've closed his eyes without fear of losing the path.

* * *

John Russell hid inside the trunk of a hollow oak. Cobwebs clung to his hair where he stood in the darkness of that missing heartwood. He was still breathing heavily from his run when it occurred to him something was wrong.

At first he couldn't explain the strange apprehension creeping over him. He stood listening.

Dead quiet.

Then he realized what it was—the woodpecker had fallen silent. He'd heard its steady knocking at some besieged trunk since he'd entered the forest and now it had ceased of a sudden.

Someone was in the woods.

He heard a rustling in the brush, coming closer. It reeked like a dead thing, putrid, foul, and the smell ripened until he knew it was standing just outside the hollow tree.

It scratched at the trunk.

He began to shake. He'd had no fear during his crazed descent along the switchbacks and he'd come to care little whether he lived or died, but standing there with the stench of the beast choking him, he wanted to howl in terror.

He could hear breathing. A low eager sound deep in its throat.

Then footsteps approaching at a run. The beast growled and withdrew, its smell lessening until John Russell could breathe without gagging.

A hand shot through the opening of the trunk and jerked him outside.

* * *

The boy tripped on an exposed root and landed at Carnoviste's feet outside the hollow tree.

Carnoviste let go of him. He stood over the boy, shaking his head.

Zunde and Pericho came crashing through the undergrowth.

"Let's whip some sense into him," Zunde said.

The boy lay staring at the ground. The warriors

followed his gaze and saw the tracks he studied. The left hindpaw was malformed, twisted inward. They watched a blade of grass crushed in one of the prints spring back upright.

"Bear," Carnoviste said. "You're lucky he didn't eat you."

Zunde's eyes darted from tree to tree. "Go away, Grandpa," he said, the People's customary response when they encountered a bear.

Carnoviste offered the boy his hand. He took it and rose.

"If he belonged to me, I'd tan his hide good," Zunde said.

Carnoviste looked at the boy. "It's dangerous to go wandering these woods by yourself. Especially without a bow. Maybe it's time we made you one, uh?"

The boy stared, uncomprehending.

Carnoviste slapped him on the shoulder. "Let's find that mule and go home."

"Better hope the bear didn't eat it," Zunde told them. "That's old Taklishim's mule and he'll be mad as a hornet. Then this boy will wish it ate him up too."

* * *

They rode down the banks and found the mule drinking from the river. "Ride him home," Carnoviste told the boy, motioning at the mule.

The boy got down from behind Carnoviste. He felt drained, weary after the flood of adrenaline, and despairing under the acceptance of defeat. He mounted the mule and headed back with the warriors.

Returning along the river they encountered the medicine man. He was leading his own mule from the pines.

"Out alone?" Carnoviste said. "That's risky. There's a bear in these woods."

"I've been hunting silver sage," Nantan said. "I needed it for a ceremony."

"Will you sing over me?" Zunde asked. "The boy led us across the bear's trail and I don't want to get the sickness."

It was a belief among the People that bear sickness caused foaming at the mouth, exhaustion, and deformities. Only a medicine man with Bear Power could cure the suffering.

Nantan had possessed such Power since his youth. One day when he was a young man, a grizzly attacked him, scarring his face and laming his foot. The story of how he'd killed the bear with his rifle was a favorite around the campfire.

"Don't worry," he told Zunde. "My song will protect you."

The warrior looked relieved. "I'll steal something good for you on the next raid."

Nantan nodded at the boy. "Did he try to escape?"

"He just went exploring," Carnoviste said, "and wandered too far. Now he knows the danger."

The medicine man grunted. He mounted up and they returned to Pa-Gotzin-Kay.

* * *

They ate mesquite beans and acorns and dried wild berries and whatever game the hunters brought in. When a deer was killed, everyone shared the meat. Nobody went hungry so long as any of them had food.

The inhabitants of Pa-Gotzin-Kay were for the most part Chiricahua. However, clan distinctions held little importance to those forest rebels who were so few in number in these dread latter days. The men were short with wide shoulders and thick chests. They valued their women for strong bodies and good humor. Their children were greatly indulged. The captive boy never saw a parent strike their child even in discipline, laughing instead when a boy or girl did something wrong, making fun of them, saying, "Don't you know better? We don't do such things. That isn't the way of the People."

Gathering piñons or berries, the wives and maidens always went in parties. Warriors never hunted without companions. They were a gregarious lot who found solitude intolerable and many of the grown men among them hadn't spent a night alone their entire lives—save during their boyhood vision quest. Only Nantan was known to slip away on occasion, a task required by his Power.

The boy had a difficult time acquiring the language. It was tonal and unwritten and different pitches of a single word might communicate diverse meaning. His daily immersion sped up the learning process, but it remained hard fought.

They scorned profanity. Insults were based solely on character.

They considered it rude to address a person by name to his or her face. Titles and endearments were used instead, unless the one in question wasn't present. The names of the dead went unspoken for fear of beckoning their spirits from the Other World where they might be hunting or dancing, angry at being called back to the realm of the quick.

The People looked upon nothing with more outrage than incest, the one social offense never countenanced under any circumstances. First practiced by Coyote, it was spoken of in a lowered voice or else the topic simply avoided. There was no ceremony against it or to cleanse the lingering effects and those found guilty were marked until death.

Closely linked with incest, witchcraft was also cause for grave concern. A witch was someone who used Power for harm and caused torment or sickness. If it was known a victim had been slain by means of witchcraft, an avenger of the blood was justified in slaying the witch in turn.

Each morning prayers ushered the sun. A Power they couldn't define pervaded every rock and spring, every tree and animal. Their contract with that elemental world was instinctive, unconscious, and the People were absorbed in mystic seasons and daily magic.

Planting, gathering. Hunting and harvesting. When the mountain animals were fat, the warriors departed for the hunt. Boys too young for the true hunt carried home rabbits and quail and packrats for the stewpot. Women harvested piñon pine nuts, mescal, and the fruit of the prickly pear. Ripening seasons determined the rhythm of their migrations, following each harvest to different elevations of the Blue Mountains.

After his attempted escape the boy was watched carefully. Carnoviste seemed to notice him at last, no longer ignoring him. They were crafting a bow out of a green piece of mulberry and Carnoviste made him understand they'd go hunting after it was finished. The boy was permitted to practice with an old bow until his was ready.

Neiflint and Oblite were visibly jealous of the time their father spent with him. They gave the boy hard looks and called him yodascin, born outside.

Carnoviste showed him how to grip the bow, resting the arrow on his thumb on the bow's left side while his right hand pressed the neck of the arrow to the string. He showed him how to make long shots holding the bow crossways and raising it high.

The boy stood in the pasture loosing arrow after arrow into a deadfall he'd dragged from the woods. At his every miss Oblite and Neiflint writhed in exaggerated laughter. "A blind maiden could make a better shot," Oblite called. Finally his lack of reaction bored them and they went off to play.

Left alone, his practice was relentless. After a while his arms grew strong and he started hitting the round knot on the deadfall. His skill was improving, but he'd never be a master like Carnoviste. The boy watched, stunned, as the chief loosed seven arrows in the sky before the first could hit the ground.

A light snow fell and covered the plateau with a pale blanket. They had to break the ice those mornings Carnoviste led them to the pool. Running back up the banks their bare feet crunched snow. They stood quivering, close to the fire, soaked and miserable.

Each day the boy checked his bow's progress, the mulberry curved by a length of sinew tied to either end, drying in the sun. At last on the eighth day Carnoviste told him it was ready.

* * *

The night before the hunting trip a band council was held.

Warriors and old men assembled about the fire. In the

outer circle the boy sat with the women and children. Already he could understand much of what was said. Ishton was helping him with the language and every day he made new strides.

Before the council began, he'd heard some boys talking. Zunde was angry, they whispered, and might challenge Carnoviste for the title of war chief.

Zunde was bold to contest Carnoviste's fitness to lead. The issue at hand, causing some division between the warriors, had its roots in the boy's captivity. Following Carnoviste's recommendation they were staying on Pa-Gotzin-Kay instead of wintering in the foothills. Hard months lay ahead. Pestilence had wiped out the crops they'd planted earlier in the year and there wasn't enough food to last a long winter. Zunde headed up the faction in favor of descending where the weather wasn't so harsh and cattle were nearby for the taking. The People thought it tame and spiritless to accumulate slowly by the sweat of the brow what could be got quickly through the loss of a little blood.

Common election would determine the council's decision. Those who opposed its verdict weren't bound by the will of the majority, democracy's mob rule, but could pursue the path of their choosing. The individual remained sovereign.

Carnoviste spoke first. "You all know my thoughts. It's death for us so close to the valley. The Mexicans want revenge for the kidnapping. We must hold off raiding for a time and stay where our children are safe. Hear my brother out, but don't forget the danger."

Ishton sat listening to her husband, proud of his confidence in knowing what was right for the People. These were uncertain days, but she believed his judgement was true.

Then it was Zunde's turn.

"Look at your fields," he told them. "What have we grown? A few potatoes and turnips we'll eat in a half moon. The stock will be scrawny on winter grass. When we go hungry, the little ones will suck the marrow from old bones. Your war chief says hide on our mountain and starve like cowards. I say we take what we want from our shepherds in the valley. Make them pay for everything they've stolen. If they fight back, we'll kill them in their fields and pastures and mud-walled villages."

The younger braves cheered his speech. Zunde sat down.

The hails of approval woke a fear in Ishton. She hadn't known so many supported Zunde's ambitions.

Carnoviste rose again and addressed the council. "My brother speaks like thunder, but I speak to you like lightning. He tells you winter will be hard. Nothing's so hard as the loss of a son or daughter. This is a good place to live, a happy place. Our stock will last. The game's still plenty—the Mexicans haven't killed every deer or cut all our woods yet. I won't allow any child to go hungry. If it comes to a raid, I'll lead it myself, but I won't endanger the lives of our women and little ones so a warrior can grow fat on plunder."

Zunde's face remained expressionless.

Carnoviste looked them over. "My People, the choice is yours," he said and sat down.

Ishton saw the old man rise slowly to his feet, the grandfather whose mule the boy had taken. Taklishim stood before the council. He was the eldest among them and respected by all.

"Oh, friends," he said. "Listen to an old man and his mistakes. Before you decide this matter, hear what I have to say. Once I was young and strong as you are now. I was happiest when raiding and killing and driving off horses. The elders called me a fine warrior. My lodge was always filled with hides and wonderful things to eat. My wives gave me four sons. They grew up strong and so fast. They became good raiders, perfect shots. They said, You grow old and sit here by the fire and dream your dreams and we'll take care of you when you can't climb on a horse anymore. Friends, listen to me."

Tears shone in Taklishim's eyes. "I was pleased. I looked forward to many pleasant winters. One after another my sons went forth on the war path and one after another they didn't come home. Two of my wives were also killed by the White Eyes, a third died of a fever, and she who remains is old and feeble like myself.

I'm blind and helpless. We depend on you, our friends, for what we eat and wear and for a place by the fire. This is an unhappy way to live. But if there had been no war, then today I'd be in my own lodge with my sons and grandsons and my women, all of us warm and content. I don't care if winter here will be hard. You who've talked against peace, think long and take back your words. What war has done to me it will surely do to you."

The old man sank back down and stared into the fire.

Ishton felt as though her heart would break for Taklishim's sorrows.

"His words are my words," Carnoviste said.

Once more Zunde rose. "I've heard talk and more talk, but nothing's ever done. Good words don't raise horses and cattle. Good words don't restore my grandfather's warm springs. Good words don't stop our People from dying."

He stood with arms crossed. "I'm tired of talk that always comes to nothing. It makes my heart sick to hear good words."

* * *

The snow told stories. Carnoviste and the boy walked morning parklands and mesas where the blankets lay deep. They wore their heavy coats and they carried bows and studied the tracks. A place where deer walked

171

and fed and played. A place where the prints of wolves crossed those of a coatimundi. All of them hunting in their way for something to fill their bellies.

Against the protests of Neiflint and Oblite, Carnoviste had allowed only the boy to accompany him. He needed lessons in which the younger pair were already well-versed. Their superior skill would daunt the older boy, Carnoviste believed, and so the brothers stayed home.

They came to where a mountain lion had leapt upon a doe in the night and ate his fill, then the lion dragged his leavings off and partly covered it with loose brush.

"He hasn't gone far," Carnoviste said. "His stomach's satisfied. He'll be sleeping close by."

Carnoviste had brought his Springfield. It was his intention to use only bows, desiring to teach the boy in the old ways, but if they stumbled upon the mountain lion in an ill-temper, his rifle was hanging from its shoulder-strap.

They continued on and entered the woods. A raven lighted on a hackberry bough and cawed at them and waved black wings.

"I've known a crow to lead wolves or even hunters to game they want killed," Carnoviste said. "Sometimes birds will try to tell us something. Like they used to when the People, the trees, and four-legs all talked the same language."

The raven sailed out over the trees.

"If a crow ever leads you to game, make sure you thank him and leave plenty for him to eat."

Afternoon found them at the edge of an oak grove watching a small herd of deer. The herd stood eating wildberries. For a long time Carnoviste and the boy lay hidden in thick brush.

"Patience is the hunter's sharpest weapon," Carnoviste whispered.

The sun was coming out of the clouds, snow starting to melt under their bodies, and now the deer moved closer. They were mule deer and the light shone on their browncolored hides.

The boy slowly nocked an arrow. The shaft was grooved with lightning marks to prevent the wood from warping and to act as bloodgutters. He'd filed the metal arrowhead to a sharp point.

He eyed a heavy-beamed buck. Perfect antlers, not a single tine broken in combat with rivals during the season's rut. Muscles rippled under his coat when he moved.

The boy recognized the depth of the open world in the buck's face. Immortal because he couldn't see the end, death long behind him and God in front. That outward gaze was pure and direct, a will-less knowing.

When the buck was standing broadside and in range, the boy took a slow breath. He waited for the buck to drop his head, then he raised the bow, drawing the string back, and aimed and loosed the arrow.

It pierced the buck. Does and fawns scattered, leaping stiff-legged through the trees. The buck ran impaled with the plumed shaft of his fate.

Carnoviste and the boy rose. They trailed the drops of blood and hoofprints through the woods and after a while they found the buck where he lay dead in the dappled light.

* * *

They cut the venison into strips and spread them on brush to dry in the sun. Smoke from a constant fire kept the flies away.

Waiting for the meat to be ready for packing they were camped two days in the Blue Mountains. The weather remained clear. Carnoviste taught him to make fire with a notched stick and how to tell whether an observed animal was going toward or away from water.

Around the fire at night they were quiet, watching sparks borne on the wind vanish in darkness. Then Carnoviste would speak of the old people in days long passed but somehow still present in those mountains. What their lives had been like, their struggles and sorrows. The boy let him talk and asked no questions. He sat listening until Carnoviste fell silent again and it was time for sleep.

Near the camp was a low place where water seeped

from a wall and collected. When they first kneeled to drink, the boy stared down at his image in the pool. Carnoviste reached over and troubled the water and the reflection disappeared.

"Always stir it up before you drink," Carnoviste said. "It's not good to look into the water."

The boy nodded. He brought his cupped hands to his lips and drank.

When the meat was ready, they pounded it smooth enough to pack easily in the cowhide bags, then mounted and started back toward Pa-Gotzin-Kay. That afternoon they were passing along the base of a hill when Carnoviste paused. On the crest stood a crude wooden scaffold, pine branches lashed with strips of rawhide.

"Stay here," he told the boy.

Carnoviste rode up the hill. He circled the sky burial platform.

"Bring me a blanket," he called.

The boy rode to the crest and handed over the blanket. Carnoviste spread it across the platform. He sang a medicine song, then began picking up the old bones and placing them on the blanket.

"The sky and birds have done their work," Carnoviste said. "I know a cave where the bones can rest. It's not far, we shouldn't be too late getting home."

The boy spoke in halting Apache. "Who was it?"

"A friend. Let his name go unspoken. We hunted

together in these mountains. He was a fine shot, I never saw him miss. We raised him up in honor."

Carnoviste wrapped the last of the bones in the blanket and cradled the bundle. The boy followed him down the hillside and they left the sky burial standing empty.

* * *

The council had agreed that staying the winter on Pa-Gotzin-Kay would serve the People best. It wasn't an easy choice. Many favored Zunde's desire for raiding and thought the chief showed weakness in his preference for peace.

They whispered among themselves. Carnoviste's Power had never been strong, they said. Its limit was well known—the promise he'd received in his youth during his vision quest. Four times a phantom voice had repeated that death would refuse him so long as he remained in the Blue Mountains. He hid behind this prophecy, some argued, avoiding the valley out of fear for his own life.

Carnoviste knew his experience of Power was all too limited. The guiding force he'd felt while tracking the boy, when somehow he realized death lurked in the woods, was a true anomaly for him. He'd never felt it before or since. The promise of his vision quest and a dominion over horses were his only other manifestations of Power.

He had an easy way with mustangs, but no one considered it of any consequence. A horse was nothing to hold in esteem, for they were a mountain people who rode to battle but dismounted to fight. The horse was a tool and food source, little else. In a race for his life a warrior would ride his horse to exhaustion before cutting its belly open and pulling out foot after foot of intestine to fill with water and seal at both ends. Then he'd run on with the tubular canteen coiled about his waist and shoulders, traveling almost as fast afoot as horseback. Such a culture didn't prize Carnoviste's ability to gentle mustangs.

In the end it was Nantan who'd resolved the debate.

When he voiced his support for Carnoviste, reluctant though it was, the warriors assented to his wisdom. Nantan's guidance was honored, his visions feared, and all the village respected him as one with great Power.

The boy heard strange old tales—

Mexican soldiers once trapped the People in a cluster of rocks. The warriors were out of ammo, unable to cover a retreat for the women and children, bullets whining, ricocheting in their hiding place. The soldiers kept a constant stream of fire. One desperate brave even proposed they suffocate the smallest children and make a run for it. Then Nantan opened his medicine bundle and began singing. Moments later he started vomiting forth rifle cartridges, the rounds spilling out of his mouth, pouring on the ground, enough to fill a bucket before it was finished. When the soldiers advanced on their hiding place, the People cut them down and made their escape.

On two separate occasions in his youth Nantan was shot by the White Eyes. Astonished companions saw the wounds close and heal moments after he'd suffered them, leaving his body without so much as a scar. "No mortal hand can ever slay me," Nantan said.

Everyone acknowledged the truth of his declaration. Even the foolhardiest braves were careful not to offend the Power of the immortal medicine man.

Once he'd been a warrior, as well as a shaman, but those years had passed long ago. Now age and his crooked left foot were harsh impediments. Sometimes Nantan rode out with a raiding party to bless the warriors along the journey, but he always remained in camp during the raid itself. Power alone granted him the reverence he savored so deeply.

It was Nantan who'd first nominated Carnoviste as chief. The warrior was young and courageous, well-liked by all, and Nantan had sought such a brave, one whose lack of Power insured the medicine man's authority. Nantan needed the chief for his youth and strength and the chief needed Nantan for his Power.

Zunde was furious, but he'd abide the council's decision.

* * *

The boy learned the name of the old hag who'd killed his mother—Gouyen, the wise woman—and he learned she was Nantan's twin sister and a seer in her own right.

It was Gouyen who started the rivalry between the boy and her brother's slave. She bragged of Nantan's slave, the Nakaiye or captured Mexican boy, the one who'd been crying at the spring, Gouyen boasting that he was a strong fighter. They called the slave Coyote. She swore no other boy could beat him and soon she'd talked up a fight.

The People loved to gamble on races and feats of skill and endurance. A contest between two captives was natural enough, but the old woman speeded things along, telling anyone who'd listen how Coyote could whip the White Eye boy. Some of the braves argued with her. Sure, Coyote outweighed him, but the White Eye was stubborn—he'd tried to run away through the woods and they didn't think he'd give up so easy in a fight.

Odds were discussed, bets made. They sent one of Bihido's wives to fetch the White Eye boy from the pasture where he was practicing archery.

"Your master wants you," she said.

He lowered his bow. "What does Carnoviste need me for?"

She stood with arms crossed, looking the boy up and down, assessing some unknown quality.

"You're small," she said. "You better be tough. Don't disappoint us."

He didn't know what she was talking about.

She led him out to the place where a crowd had gathered in a wide circle. Neiflint and Oblite stood by their father and their mothers Tsaltey-koo and Hanlonah. The boy looked for Ishton, but she wasn't there.

Across the circle the medicine man watched him approach and he called to his sister. Gouyen stepped forward gripping their slave's arm. She started greasing her champion with animal fat, smearing the stuff over his shoulders, and she whispered something in his ear.

Coyote stared the boy dead in the eyes and the boy knew it was going to be bad.

He stepped up to Carnoviste. "What did you need me for?"

"I bet a horse and blankets on you. Fight him and win."

Tsaltey-koo held a gourd bowel. "Take off your shirt," she said.

He hesitated, then did as he was told. She scooped a handful of fat from the gourd and rubbed her hands in it and slathered it across his chest.

"If you whip him," Carnoviste said, "I'll give you Nantan's mustang pony."

When she finished greasing him, he followed Carnoviste out into the center of the circle. Gouyen led Coyote forward.

Carnoviste's words of advice were brief. "Don't let him whip you," he said, then walked away and left the boy to face his opponent.

Someone shouted and immediately Coyote rushed him. The boy dodged. Then they were circling, hunched low, moving around the ring of watchers.

Coyote charged again and grabbed him, wrapping both arms around the boy's legs, his chest close against him, going for the takedown. Off-balance, the boy tried to break loose, but then Coyote was lifting him up and he came slamming down on his back in the grass. He struggled to keep Coyote from pining him.

He twisted free and rolled and came up on his knees, trying for a reversal. He grabbed Coyote's right arm, strained to pull it into a lock. Too much grease, not enough leverage—Coyote slipped out of his grasp.

They grappled and broke holds.

The crowd yelled. There was a loud boo from those who'd placed wagers on the boy when Coyote got a controlling position, then the boy broke free again to the sound of cheers.

Coyote dove crosswise over him and gained side control.

The boy lay face-up, his shoulders off the ground, and twisted under his heavy opponent, fighting back with all he had, muscles straining.

Rage in Coyote's eyes. Something else there as well. A burgeoning desperation at the fact the boy still refused to yield.

"Give in, you coyote," the slave told him, speaking without thought, using his own name as insult. Then he realized what he'd said and the fury in his gaze flared.

Coyote moved, making the transition from side control to a mount. The boy knew he'd be finished, pinned for good, unless he acted now.

He shot out an arm and entangled Coyote's right leg, holding him off, and brought his own leg up and around. He hooked his legs behind Coyote's back, ankles locked together in a closed guard, restricting his opponent's movement. It meant Coyote needed to pass the guard, force the boy to release his grip. He could've dug his forearm into the boy's inner thigh, the pain compelling him to let go, but there was a stark and growing fear behind Coyote's anger, clouding all his thoughts.

So he balled a fist instead and struck the boy hard in the face.

Blood ran from his nose. The rules of the match were broken now, cast aside, and he wasn't the one who'd violated them.

Nobody rushed in to pull them apart. Coyote had forfeited, but the fight was far from over. A fighter had performed with dishonor, yet the People understood that true struggles for life and death played by no rules and later enemies would prove themselves more treacherous indeed. To claim victory the boy would have to gain the upper hand alone.

Coyote punched him again.

The boy released his ankles in an open guard. Coyote grinned—and he started into a mount, ready to pin the boy's shoulders.

The boy braced his right hand against Coyote's neck for leverage and brought his left leg up. He positioned his foot against Coyote's knee. Then it was over in an instant, the boy shoving Coyote's knee out from under him, sweeping him down onto his back.

He rose gripping Coyote's wrist, wrenching it in a submission hold. Coyote started to get up. The boy bent his wrist back ever so much and Coyote dropped down fast.

Their audience was whistling, cheering, even the ones who'd bet on Coyote. Carnoviste watched with his arms crossed, silent as stone.

The boy stood over his enemy and wiped blood from his nose.

Coyote looked up with pleading eyes. "Let go," he begged. "Please. You win."

The boy stared. "I'm no coyote," he said. Then he jerked his enemy's wrist back hard.

It snapped and Coyote screamed. He lay grasping his broken wrist, howling in pain.

Gouyen turned and walked away from the crowd.

When the boy stepped forward, he was met with cheers and whistles, the People crying champion, and Carnoviste picked him up and carried him on his shoulders.

* * *

The grass rippled in low winter light, rising up from a thin bed of fresh snow. The boy sat on the deadfall at the pasture's edge. He held a cane arrow and fitted the end with fletchings of turkey feathers and when he glanced up, Ishton was walking toward him.

She sat down beside him and held out a single golden feather. "I found this by the spring. I thought you'd want it."

"Thank you," he said and took the feather.

Their breath plumed in the chill air.

"It's from an eagle," she told him. "They're the best for arrows. You know why?"

He shook his head.

"An arrow with eagle feathers can never miss. It's a special Power that finds the heart every time."

She looked across the pasture where Carnoviste was stepping up to the wild pony he'd won from Nantan, the boy's prize. It was well known the mustang had bitten Taza's stallion, taking a chunk of flesh out of him before galloping away. The bay pony was skittish and mean, beautiful and fast. Nantan thought he'd played a fine joke on the chief, wagering a horse that couldn't be ridden, a beast he'd intended to butcher and eat, but he'd forgotten Carnoviste's Power Over Horses.

The horse shied from him. Ears pricked, nostrils flaring. Carnoviste held a reata, twirling the loop slowly, moving closer.

He cast the loop over the horse's head and tightened it fast, choking the mustang, driving him to the snow, and stood gripping the reata.

The boy was glad he was too far away to hear the horse's frenzied breathing.

Only when it seemed the mustang neared the point of death did Carnoviste slacken the loop.

"He's proud of you," Ishton said. "You know that?"

The boy stared across the plateau.

After a while the mustang rose and stood trembling in a full lather. However ruthless his methods, however callous his treatment, Carnoviste was a man who loved horses and like all such men he was careful never to break their spirits. To do so would dishonor his own Power.

Carnoviste passed a hand over the mustang's eyes and stroked his ears and forehead. Then he placed his mouth over the mustang's nose and breathed softly into his nostrils. Breath to breath, man and beast.

"He's a good father," Ishton said. "The best. You see how he cares for his sons, Tsaltey-koo's and Hanlonah's boys. I hope soon to bear a son for him."

The boy didn't have any reply for her.

"No one loves these mountains more than him," she went on. "There's so much freedom here. Everything he does is to keep the People free."

Carnoviste tied a thong around the horse's lower jaw. He mounted up without protest and rode bareback across the plateau. When he stopped before them, he was grinning.

"You whipped that coyote good," he told the boy. "Nantan won't bet against us again anytime soon. You want to ride?"

He climbed down and stood holding the thong.

The boy rose and stepped forward.

"You have to show him there's no reason to be scared," Carnoviste said.

The boy rubbed the horse's nose, rubbed his head and ears as he'd seen Carnoviste do. He hesitated.

"Go ahead," Carnoviste said. "Let him know who you are."

The boy leaned in close and held his palms over the pony's eyes and blew into his nose.

When he climbed on, the horse didn't try to throw him. He rode out through the snowy grass. Carnoviste and Ishton sat on the deadfall side by side and watched as the sun withdrew behind a silhouetted ridge to the west. The horse and rider passed before the sunset and passed across the bed of fallen snow and they moved as a singular dark form against the wine-colored light.

CHAPTER EIGHT

It was the longest winter of Jubal's life.

At first he tried to sleep away the grief and fear, but no dreams of better days would come—only nightmare, the horror relived afresh each night.

So he spurned sleep and took up the bottle instead. Drink consumed his waking hours. He ate little, became gaunt and thin. Sunken cheeks, hollow eyes.

His son was alive and his son was dead. The waiting took him out to the limits of endurance, to the place where he had nothing left, not for himself or any other, not even his baby daughter.

Dolores found him in the courtyard late at night smoking cigarettes and sipping whiskey. Lost in his own powerlessness. She listened to his soft curses. "Gut-eaters, savages…"

She watched this man she loved change into another person, a stranger among them, and the transformation ripped her heart out.

He got drunk and punched a window, shattering the pane and cutting himself, bleeding all over the floor. He got drunk and took a swing at Hector when the segundo suggested he'd had enough. He got drunk and walked up to the family cemetery on the hill and passed out on his wife's grave. Waking there in the harsh light of morning, a blazing sun that seemed to throw fistfuls of fire ants in his eyes.

Never once did he raise his voice to Dolores or Claudia, never laid a hand on them in anger. Nor would he turn Dolores away when she asked for help continuing the studies Sara had begun with her, but he was an indifferent teacher. Once he'd finished teaching her the rudiments of reading and writing in Spanish, the girl was left to her own devices to puzzle out an education. She also wished to master speaking English. Though Jubal helped her with this, she found that Wesley was easier to talk to.

For the most part Hector saw to the daily business of the ranch. Dolores took care of the young girl and the house work. Jubal stopped shaving and his beard grew long and unruly and he was like a ghost they lived with all that December and into the new year. This pale revenant that was once a father.

Adela worried over them. She cooked dishes he'd once relished, old favorites. Nights around the dinner table he pecked at his food and held Claudia in his lap, talking to her while she ate, but his eyes were distant. Dolores knew he wasn't really there. Absent as a disciple of Swedenborg, his mind searching the sierras pinnacle and vale while down below his body cleaned and repaired itself, forgotten flesh.

* * *

The McKenna family's tragedy caused a panic in the valley. Villagers and farmers went about armed, carrying whatever weapons they possessed, and no one dared travel alone or remain on the road once night had fallen.

Recent years had seen occasional violence from bronco Apaches, but nothing like this. When word crossed into Arizona, the *Douglas Daily Dispatch* seized on the story. Their articles describing the last wild Indians and the kidnapping of an Anglo boy sent the border into turmoil.

Newspapers across the United States took notice. Fred Winn, supervisor of the U.S. Coronado National Forest, shared his personal theory with reporters. According to Winn, the Apache chief could be none other than Charlie McComas, the judge's little boy now a bloodthirsty killer. In 1886 renegade Apaches attacked the McComas family on the Silver City-Lordsburg road, murdering the judge and his wife and carrying young Charlie away. Phantom sightings of a blond savage had been made from time to time ever since.

1929—

Before the year is out Charles Lindbergh will complete the first nonstop flight from New York to Paris. Color television is demonstrated to the public, images of a bouquet of roses and an American flag. Surrealist René Magritte paints *The Treachery of Images,* Hubble announces his observation of the expanding universe, and on a Tuesday in October the New York Stock Exchange crashes.

The annual reunion of the Trail Drivers Association is held in San Antonio. Hunched old men in John B. Stetson hats pose for photographs beside silver-haired Comanches in suits and ties. Meanwhile theater marques around the world advertise cowboy and Indian movies.

The kidnapping of John Russell McKenna is featured as a *Ripley's Believe It or Not* cartoon.

* * *

Colonel Emilio Sanchez, commandant of the military barracks at Agua Prieta, dispatched a motorcycle courier to the McKenna ranch. The courier departed riding a Triumph Type H, its sidecar mounted with a machinegun. When at last he arrived at the remote ranch some days later, it was on the back of a mule and the courier's haggard appearance was much the worse for wear. He presented the colonel's letter to Jubal McKenna.

Jubal looked over the sealed envelope.

"You like whiskey?" he asked the man.

They sat on the porch. He poured them both a glass,

then broke the seal on the envelope with a letter opener and withdrew the contents and began reading.

After expressing his deepest sorrow for the McKenna family's tragedy, Sanchez offered the services of his federal troops. His men were well-armed and highly trained, prepared to "reek bloody vengeance against the heathen devils." The colonel assured Jubal he had total authority to begin the operation without referring the matter to Mexico City.

Jubal imagined a large force of soldiers, perhaps even artillery—God help us, he thought—blundering through the sierras and endangering John Russell. When it was time to go after the boy, Jubal would need local guides from villages in the foothills. The people of the country hated federal troops. For a certainty no one would help the man who'd inflicted the army's drunken thieves and rapists on them.

Jubal took up pen and paper. He thanked the colonel for his generosity, then declined the offer as politely as possible. The next day and many drinks later the courier set out with his response.

That night Jubal lay wide awake, his mind going over the possibilities. Hungry for publicity, the colonel might try something stupid and drastic. Irrevocable disaster never seemed more likely.

Come morning he wrote the governor in Hermosillo. He explained the danger in which his son would be placed if an assault was launched too soon and his letter requested the issue be left in his hands alone. Jubal sent a vaquero to post the letter.

In a few short weeks he got his reply.

A commission was sent from the capital, signed by the governor and countersigned by various federal authorities. It granted Jubal full sanction to kill or capture all members of the renegade Apache band hiding in the Sierra Madre. The Sonoran Government would also supply a force of his choosing with arms, ammunition, and mounts to attempt the boy's rescue at such time as he deemed auspicious.

* * *

One afternoon Dolores was sitting on the porch reading to Claudia from a book of Spanish fairy tales. It was late January, but a warm day in the valley nonetheless and neither of them wore a coat.

When she glanced up from the book, she saw a horseman coming up the orchard road. In the distance she couldn't recognize him.

"Let's go inside," Dolores told the girl. She led Claudia into the empty hacienda.

From a rack in the hall she picked up the shotgun and broke it open to check that it was loaded. She didn't know where Jubal was. Passed out drunk somewhere, more than likely. A few of the vaqueros were still in the bunkhouse, little work for them this time of year, but it didn't occur to her to call for help.

"Stay here," she told Claudia. "I have to go see who it is."

She stepped back outside with the shotgun in her arms.

Men were always passing through, hunting work. Jubal's instructions were clear—never let a stranger in the yard without invitation. Anyone seeking work knew to wait for permission before they approached the house. If they crossed the yard without asking, they were looking for something else.

It was in her blood to kill to protect her own and the training of her youth wasn't forgotten. She gave no thought to scaring off a trespasser, too risky, better instead to make the first shot count.

The rider approached the yard and halted. He looked at her standing barefoot on the porch and he took off his hat in greeting, a young man with bright eyes and a wide grin.

"Remember me?" he asked. "Last time we saw each other, you couldn't speak Spanish, but I bet you learned fast."

Now she recognized the young vaquero, the one who'd made her laugh the day Jubal brought her home, the same vaquero who'd left the feast with his angry companion that night.

"You've been gone a long time," she told him. She kept her grip on the shotgun and looked him full in the eyes.

"I was hoping I could see the boss about that," he said. "Is Señor McKenna home?"

"I never knew your name."

"Angel Ochoa. Yours?"

"I'm Dolores McKenna." She lowered the shotgun and leaned it against the wall. "Come on up, Angel Ochoa. You can wait in the shade."

When Jubal returned that evening, he found Dolores, Claudia, and the vaquero all sitting on the porch steps. They shared a chocolate bar, laughing and talking.

Jubal crossed the yard and stared at Angel.

"Señor McKenna," Angel said. He rose and offered his hand.

They shook.

"What brings you back this way?" Jubal asked.

"I'm looking for work, sir."

"What kind of work?"

"Whatever I can get," Angel said.

"Good luck to you."

"I'm sorry about your wife and boy. I cried when I heard what happened."

Jubal looked him in the eye. "Where's your cousin?"

"Isidro? He's in prison."

"You didn't want to join him?"

Angel shook his head. "I never should've left this place."

"You're right about that. You might try the Babicora. I doubt they're hiring now, but they'll have something for you in the spring."

"All right," he said. "I understand."

Jubal glanced over at Dolores. She was intent, staring as though she were trying to burn a hole through him. Jubal sighed and shook his head. "Fine, let's try it one more time. Go find a bunk. You know what I pay."

"Thank you, sir," the vaquero said. "I won't disappoint you again."

Dolores gave Jubal a smile. She rose and took Claudia by the hand and went back inside.

"I don't think it's me you have to worry about disappointing now," Jubal told the vaquero.

* * *

A creek called Rojas served as the western boundary between the McKenna range and two neighboring outfits. The fences in that area were forever tearing down. Rain runoff out of the foothills fed into the little stream and the swollen torrent washed away fence posts and barbed wire. A flood the previous fall had so engorged the creek it altered its course and took out a stretch of fence three miles long. In the aftermath cattle roamed looking for green grass, heedless of invisible borders.

In mid-February Jubal rode out with a wagon and crew for an early roundup and they crossed the western division. Each ranch along the creek was expected to send vaqueros to help with the work, gathering cattle that had wandered over the downed fenceline, and any calves or yearlings would be branded according to the ownership marks on their mothers. All weaned calves without a brand were mavericks, their ownership falling to the rancher on whose land they were found.

They assembled at a line camp belonging to Los Gatos, the second largest outfit in the valley. The camp was just an old cabin and pole corrals, abandoned headquarters for one of the small ranchos the syndicate had bought up. Los Gatos was owned by a consortium of investors out of Hermosillo, wealthy financiers who'd never set foot on the property, men for whom the land was no more than an entry in a ledgerbook.

Weeks earlier Jubal met with the Los Gatos foreman and requested use of the camp's corrals. The foreman told him he didn't see any problem with that. "How many vaqueros can you send?" Jubal had asked.

"We're a little shorthanded right now," he said. "But we'll have somebody down there to cut the bunch."

It went against Jubal's idea of old-time roundup ethics—no crew, no cut. He guessed the beancounters in Hermosillo didn't approve of such early work. There was a moment when he thought about making an issue of it, but he was content with using their corrals and he decided to let it go.

After setting up at the line camp that morning, the vaqueros rode off and began hazing cattle out of the brush country. Jubal threw himself into the work, grateful for something to distract his mind.

Shortly before midday they trailed a large herd to the corrals. Some of the men were heading to the wagon for noon dinner. Branding fires burned all around. Jubal broke off from the others. He sat his horse and leaned over, reaching into his boot, and pulled out a flask and unscrewed the lid and drank.

Moroni Thayne stood with an iron in his hand. The Mormon giant towered over the other men at six foot six, blond haired and blue eyed, the youngest of seven sons. The Thayne family were part of the region's sizeable community of Latter-Day Saints and Moroni's father owned the Square and Compass ranch.

Gregorio Valdez leaned on the corral, scanning the main herd. He was the Los Gatos rep sent to watch out for the brand's interests. He smoked a cigarillo and looked bored.

Jubal took a pull from the flask and glanced over the cattle they'd just brought in. His eyes held on a spotted calf. He shoved the flask back in his boot and rode into the herd. He cut the calf out, heading it toward a small bunch of cows and calves held by McKenna riders.

"Got another for us?" Angel Ochoa asked.

"It was following one of ours," Jubal said.

"Good looking little calf."

"Hungry looking," Jubal said.

"I know the feeling."

"Nestor starving you out?"

"He said I can eat a load of buckshot next time I go up to the wagon and try to hurry him."

Jubal grinned. He turned his horse and headed back for the corrals.

A moment later Angel saw Gregorio Valdez come galloping up on a sorrel. "That spotted calf got a mother here?" Valdez asked.

"The boss said it belongs to a McKenna cow."

"It came in with a bunch they found on Los Gatos range. It's going to get branded Los Gatos."

Valdez separated the calf and ran it back toward the main herd.

When Jubal saw it, he spurred his horse. He reined in and stopped the calf with Valdez behind it. "That one belongs to me," Jubal told him.

"Then show me the mother."

"It was with her earlier in the brush. I saw it following a McKenna cow, earmarked and branded."

"Maybe it's not the same calf you spotted," Valdez said. "Could be a different one."

"It's the one."

"How do you know for sure?"

"I recognized the pattern of the spots on its hide."

The men around the fires turned to watch.

Hector rode up. "What's the trouble?"

"Hector saw it too," Jubal said. He nodded to his segundo. "Tell Gregorio you know that calf. It's the same one we saw this morning."

Hector eyed the spotted calf.

"Well, is it or not?" Valdez demanded.

"If the boss says it's the calf, it's the calf."

"You'd swear by the saints you recognize it?"

He hesitated. "I couldn't swear to it either way. But the boss—"

"I'd like to see this cow," Valdez interrupted.

One more calf branded for Los Gatos wouldn't raise Valdez's wages by a centavo, but the man was loyal to his outfit, syndicate or not. The accountants wanted every added peso of capital gain for their ledgers.

Jubal shook his head. "It makes no difference one way or the other. We found that calf on my range by the split rock."

Due east of the old creekbed stood a great boulder with a crack running down its middle. As though halved by a titan's axe in some lost golden age.

"If you found it by the split rock," Valdez said, "then you found it on Los Gatos land. The river is the line— and last time it flooded, the river moved east past the rock. Which you damn well know."

The flood had cut a new passage, the stream swinging out so that the split rock now lay to its west.

"The land didn't change," Jubal said. "The rock hasn't moved an inch."

"You want the river to stay the same, but it can't. The river always changes."

"I'm branding it McKenna," Jubal said. "We both know it's my calf."

Valdez shook his head. "We don't both know that. I'm not convinced even one of us really knows it."

"You're calling me a liar?"

It was grounds for killing a man.

Valdez stared at Jubal, sizing him up. Dark unruly beard. Empty eyes, no spirit behind them. The whole valley knew his troubles and any man who got on the wrong side of him and didn't back down was truly brave or crazy.

"Like your man said," Valdez told him. "I couldn't swear to it either way."

"Maybe we'd better settle this."

Now the vaqueros all were watching, work forgotten, careless of the branding fires slowly burning out.

Valdez gave him a shrug. "If that's how you want it to be."

They swung off their saddles and stood facing each other, both of them armed, holstered pistols slung low on their hips. Hector watched in disbelief.

"Tell me again I'm a liar," Jubal said.

"All you got to do, you want to prove it's yours, show me the cow. But you're not even looking for her. Why is that?"

A dull hum in the air. Everything heightened—colors, smoke, each microsecond clocking away.

Valdez's hand dangled at his side. The cigarillo hung in the corner of his mouth. He gave Jubal a hard stare, a promise in his gaze.

Jubal ignored the man's eyes and watched his hand instead, ready for the first anticipatory muscle twitch. It wasn't true what some men said, that you could always see it coming in a man's eyes, the moment right before he made his move. Oftentimes yes, but some men's eyes held nothing save death behind them and revealed no other truth. Jubal knew this to be so with only a glance in a mirror—for his own eyes were much the same.

"You think I'm stealing from your outfit," Jubal said. "So do something about it."

Hector stepped his horse between the pair. "Over one damn calf? I'd like to take a quirt to both of you."

"Move," Jubal told him.

"Out of the way," Valdez said.

Hector spat. "I'm not going to watch a man get killed over any calf."

Then Angel and Moroni were standing on either side of Jubal. "Come on, Mr. McKenna," Moroni said in English. "Let's cool down."

Jubal allowed the men to lead him away. They went and stood against the corral and he drank from his flask.

"We're not done with this," Valdez said. "I want a judgement on that calf."

Hector nodded at Moroni Thayne. "I say you're the new wagon boss. Anybody got a problem with that?"

Valdez shook his head. Jubal didn't speak.

"Then you call it, Moroni," Hector said.

The Mormon took off his hat and tapped the brim

against his leg. He switched to Spanish. "I'm no wise Solomon. This one's got me puzzled. I know Jubal's a man of his word, but it would make things a lot easier if we could find that cow." He looked at Angel. "Maybe you and some of the boys—"

A pistol barked.

They all turned to see Jubal standing over the fallen calf, a smoking .45 in his hand. He stared across at Valdez.

The Los Gatos rider dropped his cigarillo and stamped it under a boot-heel. Then he climbed on his horse and reined about and rode off.

"What sense is there in that?" Hector asked his boss.

Jubal holstered the pistol. "Maybe next time you'll know to back up your friends."

He stepped to a fire and pulled out an iron, glowing red hot, and it steamed when he pressed the brand to the dead calf's hide.

"Well, I reckon that solves it," Moroni said.

Jubal tossed the iron down.

Hector rode up to him. "Maybe I saw the calf following one of ours. But it didn't seem too serious about it. Just because a calf's following a cow doesn't always mean so much."

"I wouldn't have cut it if I wasn't sure," Jubal told him.

Hector shook his head and rode on past.

CHAPTER NINE

Back to Babylon. Cain and Mosby rode a Greyhound bus into New York on a snowy night in January, 1929, just over a month after Cain cut ties with the Continental Detective Agency.

Python-owned newspapers had managed in large part to control the narrative of the deaths. However, a few independent papers placed full responsibility at the feet of the coal company and their Continental agents for what those reporters dubbed the Python Massacre. Local police, all in the pocket of Python Coal, questioned Cain repeatedly about the circumstances of the shooting, but they were only interested in dismissing the matter as quickly as possible. Nonetheless Cain was forced to hire an attorney when it became clear the agency refused to stand behind him. Legal expenses drained his finances.

In the end the official investigation reached its conclusion—the picketers had sparked the tragedy by beating down a Continental detective in the crush of the crowd. Edgewater, the agency man behind the machine gun, succumbed to a lingering case of shellshock acquired in the Great War, when the violence unfolding down below caused his mind to falter and he'd cut loose on the strikers. All in all, nine picketers died and thirty-four were wounded. Cain was cleared, but his time as a Continental op was finished and the agency seemed determined to make him pay for the deluge of bad publicity.

The old man put out the word—Cain and Mosby were strictly anathema. Any detective agency that considered employing their services would find themselves on the Continental's shit list, a fate few were willing to risk.

They rode the bus into Manhattan. Rather than waste their scant savings on cab fare they walked from the station out into the snow. Pale flakes drifting down, falling through a narrow gap of sky between Gotham's monoliths, a canyon of concrete and glass and steel.

They rented a pair of rooms in a Hell's Kitchen flophouse. A widow woman named O'Mara ran the place, a fat old bitty with the gift of gab and a voice like a screech owl, but what a cook she was, a fine supper included in the price of rent.

Cain and Mosby scrounged work. They pulled night duty guarding an RCA warehouse near the docks, walking to work in the dark that winter, side by side and hunched in trenchcoats, hat brims pulled low. The warehouse was a musky relic, but it held thousands of the newest radio models awaiting distribution. Cain and

Mosby passed the nights without tuning in to a radio program or any music and they never paused to think it ironic. They preferred cards and magazines or simply talking between themselves of the old days.

Both were quiet men by nature and at peace with long silences. Neither of them had family and they were accustomed to traveling from town to town, wherever the work took them, sleeping in cheap flops or motor courts. Cain had been a soldier of fortune in the decades before he joined the Continental Detective Agency. He'd gone wherever the pay was good, fighting under the banner of a greenback dollar. His boyhood was spent in the empty Texas borderland and you could hear the country in his voice. He made no attempt to disguise his hatred for the city. That seething metropolis, a mass of densely-packed humanity, held no charm for him. He compared the steel and concrete towers to great stacks of rat cages, one atop another, and the subway tunnels reeking burrows of filth and vermin. Mosby, himself still a country boy at heart, couldn't argue with the sergeant.

All night they worked, then returned at dawn to the flop and slept through morning. On their single night off they'd always choose to find a speakeasy and raise a glass. Cain's favorite toast that winter long— "To the old man. May he sleep tight down in hell tonight."

On watch between patrols Cain would read the *Times* while Mosby paged through the latest installment of *True Cowboy Adventure* or *Black Mask*. Cain read with an eye toward news of the McKenna kidnapping in Mexico, but every night he'd end by tossing the paper into the wastebasket, another disappointment.

"Still no word, Sergeant?" Mosby asked.

Cain shook his head. "I reckon the boy's lost for good."

"Wild Indins takin kids captive in this day and age—who'd have believed it?"

"You'd believe it all right," Cain told him, "if you knew them mountains. The Sierra Madre is some of the roughest country on earth. You could hide the whole damn Apache nation in there, nobody the wiser."

Days were the hardest—Cain found himself unable to sleep, even with the heavy curtains drawn over the window in his room. Time did a slow crawl. His mind moved at lightning speed, replaying the past, insomnia's captive, and he lay restless and weary. For a long time he'd had trouble sleeping for fear of the dreams that haunted him. In his dreams he battled the dead. Lost souls, faces best forgotten. Each one come to whisper the secret in his ear. Always they greeted him at the edge of consciousness, between memory and dream, and he'd come to dread the moment he nodded off, but now it seemed even that tormented sleep was denied him. He stood at his window chain-smoking and staring out through the frost on the pane. In another room a radio played low and the heat pipes in the walls of the old house let out ragged breaths.

The headaches that had plagued him these past months gradually worsened in severity and frequency, striking of a sudden, no warning, a sharp jolt of agony that left him reeling. Pain so intense the world became black before his eyes.

Finally it seemed if Cain were exiled from the land of Nod, the inhabitants of that realm had no choice but to invade his waking world.

Voices of the dead.

Cain heard them calling.

The first aural hallucination came one gray morning as he stood alone in the communal bathroom, staring into the mirror, straight razor in hand. He was shaving the slight stubble on his cheeks, never a heavy growth for him, just enough to make shaving a necessary chore, then out of nowhere he heard his name whispered.

Cain, it spoke. He recognized Aubrey's voice from the recesses of the past, his old mentor calling beyond the grave.

He stood rigid before the mirror.

Draw the blade across your throat, Cain. A faint chorus behind Aubrey's voice, a legion of echoes urging him on.

His hand trembled holding the razor.

End it now. Before it's too late, before the secret swallows you up.

The razor fell from his hand and clattered into the wash basin. Looking around the little bathroom he saw no one there and he jerked open the door and peered out into the empty hall. Was he going mad?

In the days to come he examined his thoughts for traces of insanity, keeping watch on his own mind, alert for signs of imminent betrayal.

Once more he turned to the meditation practices the old yogi had taught him. It kept the ghosts at bay, muted the Voices for a while. He concentrated on the blue dot and escaped the restless spirits with sessions running long and deep into the Zero.

Not deep enough.

In time he heard their whispers even at those primordial depths. It seemed they'd follow him down to hell itself. Louder now, hammering at the back of his mind. Whispers to howling screams.

You know what you are, they said, that old accusation.

Cain breathed. He sat cross-legged on the floor of his room, eyes closed, and focused on the blue dot.

You know the truth, whose blood runs in your veins.

"Shut up," Cain whispered to the empty room.

The son is the father's secret revealed.

"Go back to hell," he shouted, breaking position. He slammed a fist against the floorboards. "Leave me be, you sons of bitches."

Footsteps in the hall. A fist pounding on his door.

"What's a matter, Sergeant?" Mosby asked on the other side. "Who you talkin to?"

Cain sat breathing heavy. "Reckon it was a dream,"

he said. "Talkin in my sleep. Sorry to wake you up, Mo."

A silence. "Sure you all right?"

"Get back to sleep."

He was going to need strong medicine.

Cain paid a visit to Chinatown. Up and down the sidewalks merchants called out in shrill Cantonese, hawking meats and clothing and cheap cigars, all manner of trinkets, and Cain turned down narrow Doyers Street at some remove from the hustle and bustle. Tenement houses overhead. Laundries and restaurants and tea parlors lined the street. Backrooms hosted opium dens and fan-tan gambling, while down below the street, the tongs utilized a tunnel network. Hatchet men were known to rise from those depths to slash and kill before escaping back underground. Cain walked to the sharp bend in Doyers called the Bloody Angle and stepped through the entry of the Dragon Moon tea parlor.

He returned that evening to his lonely room with a pipe and lamp and the tin of pills. It wasn't his first taste of opium. He'd smoked hop in Manchuria in 1905, sampling it out of little more than curiosity, respite from the war, and through the years afterward there was the rare indulgence, never born of the desperation he felt now.

Mosby followed the otherworldly smell to Cain's door. Sickly sweet. Like the scent of a mystic flower burning.

He knocked. "Sergeant?"

"You alone?"

"Yessir."

A moment later Cain opened the door and waved him inside.

Mosby saw the lamp and pipe on the floor, then Cain got down and lay on his side and brought the pipe to his lips. Slow euphoria in his eyes.

Mosby shook his head. "It'll own you. Once it's got a holdt of you, it won't turn loose."

"One man's poison is another's medicine," Cain said.

"You do what you got to, Sergeant. But Dr. Judas Opium always turns on you in the end."

* * *

The Voices came on hard. Cain hit the pipe harder. Trips to the Bloody Angle were soon routine and he developed a daily habit, though he was careful to keep it contained. He never smoked on the job. Every night at work he powered through the Voices without succor. While he sat with Mosby in the office, it was easy to withstand, but alone on his rounds patrolling the warehouse interior, checking each door that it was locked, he'd grow increasingly desperate for dawn and a retreat to his quarters.

Only the hop gave him dreamless sleep.

The worst of it was his mounting fear that the Voices

were only outriders, harbingers of stranger things to come. Day after day he felt shadows drawing closer. He smoked and meditated, meditated and smoked.

Focus on the blue dot.

Hide in the Zero.

If the shadows found him and showed him the old secret over again, Cain feared his mind would break.

* * *

It incubated in the darkness of his skull. In time it would take the form of a single monstrous eye surrounded by tiny jutting teeth. A bump on his head, hidden under his hair, grew like the budding of some mythic horn. Yet for now in its slow beginnings the intracranial teratoma was a small thing, growing in silence along the midline of the brain, there at the pineal region, and pressing against those folds to fire demonic visions.

Such ravenous appetite. It fed on its host like a satanic foetus.

* * *

Cain put the pipe down. His room was dim behind the curtained window. He opened his wallet and took out the newspaper clipping and held it to the faint light bleeding past the edge of the curtain. He stared at the halftone image below the headline, the McKenna boy standing beside a tall rawboned man Cain assumed was his father, the pair of them in what appeared to be an orchard, smiling for the camera. He studied the image a long time and thought about the sierras.

He'd met Aubrey in those mountains in 1886. That fateful meeting led Cain to a life of order where before there had been only chaos. He'd ridden with Aubrey in search of Geronimo and his renegade band, Aubrey on a mission for the 4th cavalry with Cain tagging along, his new-found apprentice. Without those mountains he'd never have known the craft. Everything before that time was anarchy and haze. Without the sierras he would've wandered on, lost as ever, until death like a welcome companion greeted him at last.

Even now he felt their magnetic pull, those sierras of long ago, drawing him back to complete the circle, but he feared that should he return, they would be for him only mountains of madness.

He crumpled the paper in a clenched fist.

The boy was lost. Put it out of mind.

Cain removed the glass from the opium lamp and held the clipping to the flame, then dropped the burning paper into an empty mug. He watched it burn until there was only ash at the bottom of his cup.

* * *

Aural hallucinations coupled increasingly now with

flashes of visual horror. Faces of the dead, there and gone, like a single haunted frame spliced in a film roll.

His growing dependence on the opium troubled him, but he couldn't bear the thought of parting with the only peace he had left. The hop alone promised shelter from the onslaught of old ghosts.

It wasn't enough.

The shadows broke through late one night while he was making his rounds. Mosby was on the far side of the warehouse, in the office reading one of his pulps, while Cain walked alone. The headache hit him without warning. Like an icepick through the skull. He staggered and reeled, reached out to steady himself against a crate and stood breathing hard and fast as the pain subsided.

Footsteps. Soft clop of bare feet on cement.

Cain turned and faced the shadows between the high stacks of crates.

"Who's there?' he shouted.

He clicked his flashlight on. A figure stood in darkness so complete the beam failed to penetrate.

"Step out, you son of a bitch." Cain drew his sidearm.

It came lurching forward, staggering out of the dark, a shadow slowly taking on recognizable form, and Cain realized it was the Filipino boy. His face beaten to pulp, eyes swollen shut. Open bloody wounds from the bayonets so long ago.

Another shade joined him.

Cain stood in speechless horror. It was Aubrey in

his old uniform, his stomach slashed open, cradling the intestines that spilled out and dragged on the floor with each step.

The sound of running waters. Cain saw a river streaming down the warehouse floor and in the midst of the dark water the hunched silhouette of the boatman poling his craft. Beyond the waters, an enormous serpent lay writhing in agony, a multitude of horns protruding from its severed belly.

My truest friend, Aubrey called. *Help me.*

"I can't," he cried out.

Only you can do it, Cain.

"Don't ask me to, Aubrey. Please, not that."

Only you.

The dead of four continents and a dozen wars rose from the depths and gathered about him.

A faint voice in the distance, Mosby shouting his name. Running footsteps echoed in the high ceiling of the warehouse.

Cain fought to hold onto a last sliver of sanity.

Then the corpse with lidless eyes and rotten sagging flesh rose from the water and stood before him. The dead man reached out a dripping hand.

Thief, he accused. *Surrender the ring you stole.*

"It's mine," Cain whispered. "It belongs to me now."

No Cowan is worthy to wear the ring. No savage devil.

Cain fired his pistol into the watery corpse.

Three gunshots roared, three muzzle flashes, the apparitions blinking in and out of vision, then gone at last, only fading whispers.

You know what you are, they spoke as one.

Blood never forgets.

Remember.

Cain dropped to his knees.

Mosby came running up behind him, flashlight and gun in hand. "Where they at, Sergeant?" He swung his light all around. The warehouse was empty. "Who was you shootin at?"

Cain dropped the gun and pressed his palms to his ears.

Then Mosby had his arm around him. "You got to hold it together, Sergeant. Come on, let's get you your medicine."

The Voices wouldn't be silenced. Cain heeded their call.

He remembered everything.

CHAPTER TEN

For years border gossip whispered of visits between the bronco Apaches of the Sierra Madre and their subjugated brothers in the U.S. Jubal was desperate to make contact with the broncos, some way of communicating a ransom offer. He asked Dolores if the rumors were true.

She confirmed it. From time to time men would appear at the rancheria, Apaches who'd fled their reservation, wanted for breaking the law of the White Eyes.

The San Carlos Apaches were the connection, Jubal was convinced. He asked Dolores to come with him and act as translator. She told him it was no use, they'd refuse to speak on the subject, but in the end she agreed to try.

When spring arrived, they left Claudia in Adela's care and rode west out of the valley with an escort of armed vaqueros. Camping in the mountains they made no fire and the men stood watch in shifts all through the night. When they came to Moctezuma, they turned north and rode on until they reached the mining metropolis of Nacozari de García, its population some five thousand souls, thanks to the copper concerns of the Phelps Dodge Corporation. A bust of Jesús García stood in the square. The monument honored the railroad engineer who'd given his life to save the town from a dynamite explosion in 1907.

Jubal stabled their horses in a livery. They left the vaqueros at a hotel with drinking money and orders to await their return, then Jubal and Dolores boarded the El Paso and Southwestern. They rode the train north to Arizona.

* * *

In Douglas, the American town across the line from Agua Prieta, Jubal treated Dolores with a visit to a dress shop, much against the girl's protests. Her clothes were fine, she insisted, and she knew how to mend old things—there was no need for the wasted expense. Jubal wouldn't hear of it. He said it would be a late addition to her birthday presents. They'd celebrated the girl's fifteenth birthday a week earlier, two years to the day Jubal found her injured at the spring. Because she'd no way of knowing the exact date of her birth, they'd chosen to mark it each year on the day she'd joined the McKenna family.

They took a cab to the place a woman at the station recommended. When they stepped into the shop, Rudy Vallee was crooning on the radio and a woman in a stylish velvet turban browsed a rack of clothes, swaying to the music.

Dolores stood clutching his arm, terminally shy. She wore a simple gingham dress that fell to her ankles.

A young blonde greeted them. "How may I help you?" She flashed a smile at Jubal. Her hair was cut in a bob and a string of pearls dangled from her neck.

Jubal glanced at the hem of the girl's skirt, a length that would've been scandalous only a few years ago, and he got worried for a moment, thinking maybe he'd had the wrong idea, bringing Dolores here. Then he decided the important thing was for her to be comfortable, to feel like she belonged. It was her first experience of the U.S. and he was afraid if it didn't go well, she'd feel as though she'd always be on the outside, apart from everything. If she dressed like other girls her age, he hoped she'd realize she wasn't so different.

"My daughter needs a new wardrobe," Jubal said.

He expected a strange look—the dark girl was his daughter? But it didn't seem to faze the blonde.

"We've got all the best," she said.

"That's what we're lookin for. Only the best."

She smiled at Dolores. "You have such pretty eyes."

"Thank you," she said, almost a whisper.

"I'm Maggie," the dress shop girl said.

"Dolores."

Maggie offered her hand. "Dolores, why don't you come with me and we'll find out what you like?"

Dolores relinquished his arm. She took Maggie's hand and followed, a look on her face like she was headed for a firing squad.

"Whatever she needs," Jubal called. "Don't worry about the price. The money's no object."

"I'll take good care of her," Maggie said, glancing back, giving him that smile again.

* * *

Jubal ducked outside and crossed the street to a barber's. He was the sole customer and the barber seated him at once.

"Take your time," Jubal told the man. "I'm liable to have a wait."

In the chair with a hot towel over his face he found himself thinking about Maggie, her legs in the dark silk stockings, that easy smile, and he felt a stirring. Then the guilt hit him—

Sara gone only six months and he couldn't go without it long enough not to make a fool of himself and a mockery of her memory. What had he told the blonde? Money's no object. He'd never said that before in his life. What a jackass. Had that been his feeble attempt to impress her?

His beard was lathered up. The barber took a pass with the razor and nicked Jubal's cheek.

"My apologies," the man said.

"Next time try for the carotid," Jubal told him.

* * *

Freshly shaven for the first time in months, Jubal stepped into the Green Frog Café. He ordered coffee, then used the payphone.

The switchboard girl connected him to the San Carlos Reservation. He spoke with a secretary, told her who he was, what had happened to his son. Yes, she'd heard something about that business, but she didn't see what it had to do with San Carlos. He explained they'd be driving out in the morning and he'd like to meet whoever was in charge.

"I'll schedule an appointment with Superintendent Pendergast," she said. "Though I certainly can't see what you hope to accomplish."

Jubal slid into a corner booth. He poured from his flask into the cup of coffee and drank while he skimmed a newspaper. After a while he glanced at his watch and rose from the table.

"Someone cleans up nice," Maggie said when he walked into the shop.

She took his arm and turned him to face the fitting rooms. "But you're not the only one, honey."

Dolores stepped out in a straight black dress, her arms bare, the skirt ending just below her knees. She wore heels and a cloche hat.

"Isn't she a dream?" Maggie asked.

"You like it?" Jubal asked.

Dolores gave him a big grin. "I love it," she said.

"Good," he told her. "It suits you."

* * *

Jubal had an old friend in town who let him borrow his Model A. They took Route 81 north to Safford and stayed that night in the Buena Vista Hotel.

The next day found them motoring through desert country toward San Carlos.

It was the first car Dolores had ever ridden in. Jubal pushed the sedan to its limits. He looked over at her and grinned, the girl with her window rolled down, one hand gripping her cloche hat, the other reaching outside to catch the air. She turned to him, dead serious.

"We have to get one."

He let out a laugh.

"Why not?" she wanted to know. "You can afford it."

"Where would I drive it? Cow trails?"

"I'm going to have a Ford someday."

"A Ford, huh? How do you know you wouldn't like a Duesenberg or a Rolls-Royce better? They might be more your style," he teased. "Shouldn't you try them out first?"

"Don't need to," she said. "I'm a Ford girl."

He laughed again.

"What's so funny about it? We can get one, can't we?"

"It'd scare the horses," he told her.

They drove on and Dolores stared out at the passing country. Saguaros stood like candelabra, arms outstretched. Heatshimmer over the road ahead.

When they reached San Carlos, Jubal parked in front of the administrative office, a low stucco building baking under the sun. It was the forenoon and already over a hundred degrees in the shade of a few scrawny cottonwoods.

The secretary glanced up from her typewriter when they stepped inside. She wore a pince-nez and her gray hair was pulled back in a severe bun. The nameplate on her desk read Mrs. Swenson.

"Mr. McKenna?" she asked.

Jubal nodded. "Pendergast here?"

"I'll inform the superintendent you've arrived."

Mrs. Swenson rose and stepped around her desk. She paused a moment staring at Dolores, as if only now registering the fact she was Apache, taking in her clothes, the cut of her new skirt. The old woman shook her head and made a little indignant sound in her throat.

"Well, I never," she mumbled under her breath.

In a flash Dolores was an imposter, the good feeling she'd had in her new dress shattered. The thought came to her she must look absurd. On her the beautiful clothes could never be anything but a ridiculous costume,

223

someone's idea of a joke, and she cast her gaze to the floor.

Mrs. Swenson knocked on Pendergast's door.

"Yes?" a man's voice called.

She opened the door a crack saying, "Mr. McKenna is here to see you with an Indian girl."

"Show them in."

The secretary turned back to them. "You may see Superintendent Pendergast."

Dolores stepped forward. She'd walked with grace in her new heels before. Now she was unsteady, awkward under the dour old woman's scrutiny, almost stumbling when she entered the office.

* * *

"Sit down, sit down," Pendergast told them. "May I offer you a Coca-Cola?"

The superintendent was a fat man with sweat stains under the arms of his white button-down. He sported a pencil moustache and smelled faintly of lilacs. A pair of fans on his desk were going full blast, paperweights holding down a stack of files, and a movie magazine lay open to a photo spread of Ramon Novarro.

"No thanks," Jubal answered. Dolores shook her head.

They pulled out the chairs facing the desk and sat.

"Welcome to San Carlos, sir," Pendergast said. "How

may I be of service?"

"I'm guessin you've read the papers," Jubal said. "You know who I am, you know my son was kidnapped by bronco Apaches."

"I do indeed and may I offer my sincerest condolences for your loss."

"We're tryin to pass along a message. We believe the reservation Apaches have been in contact with the renegades in the sierras. My daughter was raised in those mountains and she speaks Apache. We're lookin for anyone on the rez who might've had a connection with the broncos in the past. Maybe there's somebody you can point us toward?"

The fat man seemed not to have heard him. "So this is the wild girl?" he asked, looking Dolores over. He chuckled. "Well, aren't you the little flapper."

She kept her gaze down in her lap.

"Sure you wouldn't like a Coca-Cola?" he asked again.

Dolores shook her head.

"Cat got your tongue, dear?" Pendergast looked over at Jubal. "I'm afraid you'll have a rough go of it, if she's translating for you. Not a peep out of her."

"I don't want your Coca-Cola," Dolores said. Her voice was low, seething.

"Well, I can't endure without it," Pendergast said. "Not in these hellish climes." He raised his voice: "Oh, Mrs. Swenson? One from the icebox, please."

Pendergast moved one of the fans closer toward him and mopped his brow with a handkerchief. "I must apologize for my perspiration."

Jubal stared across at the man. "That's all right. Like I was sayin, if there's anyone—"

"Nothing about my Connecticut boyhood prepared me for this Arizona weather. But we must soldier on, I suppose."

The door swung open and Mrs. Swenson stepped inside carrying a bottle of Coke.

"Ah, you're an angel of mercy, Mrs. Swenson." The superintendent reached and took the bottle.

"You're quite welcome, sir," she said, then turned and departed.

Pendergast retrieved an opener from a desk drawer and popped the bottle cap off and took a long swig.

"Delightful," he said.

"Mr. Pendergast—" Jubal began.

"Mr. McKenna, I can only imagine what you've gone through, how difficult these past months have surely been for you. We do cling to any hope, however thin it might be, in our times of desperation. I hate to be the one to inform you, but I can say with full assurance there's no communication between the Indians under my supervision and the broncos in Mexico. Entirely outside the realm of possibility."

"I've been told otherwise."

"Believe me, I'd be the first to know if such a rumor

had a shred of truth to it."

"You don't mind if we take a look around anyway?" Jubal asked. "Talk to a few people."

"I'd be positively delighted for you to see the progress we've made. These aren't the savages of yesteryear, Mr. McKenna. It's true they still cling to a handful of old superstitions, devil dancers and whatnot, all harmless for the most part. But my Indians have made great strides into modern civilization."

Pendergast leaned forward in sudden enthusiasm. Now he projected a level of energy Dolores hadn't thought possible for such a big lethargic-looking man.

"The secret," he said, "is all in how you relate to them. The circumstances of my life haven't facilitated any offspring, it pains me to say, and the Pendergast line will end with my passing. I do, however, take succor in my work. I've come to feel a certain fatherly affection for my charges, those Apaches mature in body but not in mind. Of course, I know they're really Uncle Sam's children, as are we all, but he's kindly allowed me to play a key role in their development. It's our sacred burden to educate and protect, to provide sufficient food and clothing. The least we can do after what these noble people have suffered. Only so much can be done for the older generation. It's with the youths of today that we can make a real difference. To shape a child's mind is to shape the future itself. Taken to heart, their lessons will ensure they never deviate from the proper course.

But what am I saying? You obviously know all this very well, sir. Perhaps you should be the one advising me."

Jubal was silent, his face a stone mask.

"Let me ask you something," Dolores spoke up in English. "Do you speak Apache?"

The superintendent dabbed the kerchief at his forehead. "I regret to say my workload has prevented me from taking up the study."

"Fat old fool," she called him in her former tongue.

Pendergast gave her a hesitant smile.

"It means wise leader," she said. "A term of honor."

"You know something? I believe my Indians have used that very endearment. But they said it meant mighty hunter."

"It has more than one meaning."

Jubal shifted in his chair, trying to suppress a grin. "We won't take up any more of your time. Thank you, Mr. Pendergast."

"My pleasure."

They rose to leave.

The superintendent pressed a finger to his lips. "If you're seeking information about the sierras, campsites and trails and whatnot, there's one gentleman you might consult. An ex-scout for General Crook. Perhaps he can suggest likely areas of the mountains to search for the broncos' rancheria."

"I'd like to talk with him," Jubal asked.

"I should warn you, he's a very bitter man. You won't

find much bonhomie with him. A cantankerous old coot, as they say. One of those who've rejected the future."

* * *

Jubal left his suit jacket in the car and rolled up his shirtsleeves. They wandered San Carlos on foot.

Some three thousand souls dwelled on the reservation once called Hell's Forty Acres, various tribes and bands consolidated there by the U.S. Government. The Apaches kept scattered camps, living in traditional domed huts. Jubal saw women in colorful dresses with broad skirts laboring in melon patches. Most of the men were short-haired and wore western shirts and jeans. They were small-time ranchers and farmers, or they had jobs in road construction. Still others sat in the shade each day and drank, the defeat of generations, and watched the sun down.

They followed Pendergast's directions to the ex-scout's wickiup, all about them signs of poverty and despair, and found it shadowed in a grove of cottonwoods. The old man called Dasoda-hae sat in a wicker chair under a brush awning. He sipped from a bottle and watched a flock of sparrows.

Dolores called out a greeting in Apache. "Hello, Grandfather. Is it all right if we come talk with you?"

Dasoda-hae glanced their direction, then returned his gaze to the flock. His hair fell in a braid long and white.

He was rail-thin and his polka dot shirt billowed tentlike about his chest and arms.

They hesitated, then Jubal started toward the awning and Dolores followed. The old man looked from the Apache girl to the tall White Eye and said nothing.

"I'm Dolores," the girl said. "How are you, Grandfather?"

He ignored her, more interested in his bottle and the sparrows.

"I was born in the Blue Mountains," Dolores said, "where the People are still free."

No change of expression. As though they weren't even there.

"Grandfather, I came to ask for your help."

"Tell him what happened," Jubal said.

"This man's son was taken by the wild ones. He's a good man and never mistreated the People. They were wrong to take his son."

Dasoda-hae lowered his head and stared down at the bottle in his hands. She thought he was going to nod off.

"I'll give anything," Jubal said. "Gold, guns, whatever. Tell him there's a reward if he can get a message into the sierras. I'll pay any price to bring John Russell back."

Dolores hesitated. Then she began, "He wants to pay a ransom, anything they want. If you can send a message—"

Dasoda-hae went into a coughing fit. He pressed a handkerchief to his mouth and hunched over, his body shaking, and when the spell passed, he removed the handkerchief and it was speckled with blood.

Dolores's voice was soft. "I'm sorry, Grandfather."

The old man stared at her.

"Can we help somehow?" she asked. "Do you need anything?"

He rose from the wicker chair and clutched the handkerchief and stepped past them without a word into the dark opening of his wickiup.

They stood under the awning and they could hear him coughing inside.

"He's dying, isn't he?" Dolores asked.

"He doesn't want our help," Jubal said. "Let's go."

They moved on. They tried other residents, other approaches. Dolores greeted them in Apache and they looked from her to Jubal in grim suspicion, their conversation reluctant. The reservation Apaches were aloof, withdrawn. An undercurrent of hostility to every encounter.

She would begin by asking about their lives at San Carlos, how the roundup had gone. Then she'd tell them of her childhood in the Blue Mountains. Only after they'd been talking a while would she broach the purpose behind their visit.

They passed a group of children playing and came to a drought-choked little garden. An old woman stood leaning on a hoe. Dolores hailed her and they began talking, the woman expressing the first friendly demeanor they'd encountered. She called Dolores sister and asked if the White Eye was her husband and did he treat her well? He must, the old woman reasoned, for her to be wearing such fine clothes. Dolores explained that Jubal was her adoptive father and they'd come to San Carlos seeking help. "What can I give you, Sister?" the woman said. "Just ask."

Dolores began the tale of the boy's kidnapping.

At the first mention of the wild ones, the woman shook her head in a look of sudden fear and stepped away. She turned and called to the children who ceased their play and followed her inside the wickiup.

So it went.

Beside a stock tank they approached a man who stood gripping a horse's hoof, paring it down with a knifeblade. Dolores spoke to him and he seemed amiable enough. When she asked about contacting the renegades, he let go of the hoof and straightened and met her eyes directly, never a good sign with them, and gave her a cold stare.

"Careful, girl," he said. "You go looking for the wild ones, all you'll find is an arrow in the back."

Jubal didn't understand a word that passed between them, but he felt the hatred coming off the man like ice, directed more to Dolores than himself. If Jubal hadn't been present, he sensed the situation might've gone badly for the girl.

Before the day was finished they spoke to dozens

of Apaches. Dolores offered money for anyone who could get a message to the broncos. Those willing to suffer their questions at all simply shook their heads and denied any contact since the time of Geronimo's last surrender.

Finally at sunset they returned to the car, beaten and weary, the light bleeding away in the west over miles of desolation.

"I'm sorry," Dolores told him.

"What do you have to be sorry for? If they don't want to talk, you can't make them."

She shook her head. "My grandmother told me about places like this, but I never understood till now. I didn't know people could live this way, dead inside but still walking around."

"I wish you never had to see it."

Jubal reached for the driver's door.

A rasp of a voice came from behind him—

"Take a look in there, somebody left a present for you."

He turned and saw Dasoda-hae standing in the open parking lot, standing where they'd walked only moments before. As if they'd stepped past him without ever seeing the old scout.

"You're wonderin how you missed seein me till now," the old man said, speaking English.

"I'm curious about that," Jubal said. "Got to admit."

"I made myself invisible. It's easy—you just squeeze

your eyes shut and think to yourself, I'm not here, I'm not here. But you got to believe it. There are lots of crazier things that come true when you start believin em. You believe that?"

"Can't say that I do," Jubal told him. "I think maybe you were over there—" he nodded to the superintendent's Packard across the lot "—crouched on the other side of the car. Then you stepped out after we went on by."

"I was right here the whole time. You just couldn't see me on account of I was invisible."

"All right, you were invisible. What's this about a present?"

Dasoda-hae nodded at the Ford. "Go ahead, look in the window."

Jubal looked. A rattlesnake lay in the floorboard.

He tried the sedan's doors, still locked, all the windows up and intact.

"How the hell?" he said.

"It's a keyhole snake," Dasoda-hae told him. "The kind comes in through the keyhole. Get that snake out of there, then we can go for a ride."

* * *

Jubal used a long ocotillo stalk to drag the rattlesnake out of the sedan and they left it slithering across the gravel lot. Now they were driving through the desert night, departing the reservation, the old man riding in the backseat.

"Go left up here," Dasoda-hae said.

Jubal turned onto the blacktop. He glanced back in the rearview at the reservation, wondering if Pendergast would have him arrested for absconding with one of his Indians.

"Where we headed?" Jubal asked.

"Keep goin straight. I'll let you know when to stop."

Black desert stretched around them. Empty, endless. An owl glided through the beam of their headlights.

"Bad sign," Dasoda-hae told them. "Owl crossin our path. Maybe none of us goin to make it home alive, uh?"

The old man laughed and his laughter turned to coughing. It racked his body and he pressed the handkerchief to his mouth.

They drove on. After a while Jubal saw the lighted roadhouse ahead, neon oasis, the dirt lot packed with cars. He understood it was their destination before the old man said, "My throat's a little dry. Maybe we better turn in here."

Jubal found a spot near the front of the roadhouse and parked. They could hear a western band playing inside the cinder block building. The door of the roadhouse swung open and a man stepped out, placing a straw boater on his balding head. He walked the slow deliberate walk of a drunk who knows his condition. The man climbed in a coupe and fired the engine and drove off.

"Nice place, uh?" Dasoda-hae said. "The sheriff's brother-in-law owns it. They don't let Indins inside, but they'll sell to em out the back. My feet hurt, though, and it's a long walk around there. Maybe you better go in for me."

"What do you want?" Jubal asked.

"Bottle of whiskey. I'm tired of that rotgut on the rez. I think they make it out of Gila monster piss."

Jubal eyed the place, the customers stepping out. He looked back at the old man, then turned to Dolores in the passenger seat.

"It'll just be a minute."

"I'll be fine," she said.

"Stay inside, keep the doors locked."

* * *

"Are you going to help us?" Dolores asked in Apache.

They were alone in the Ford. The sound of a fiddle and guitar came from the roadhouse. The doors opened in a burst of light and laughter and two men came striding out.

"Talk English," Dasoda-hae said. "It suits you. Kinda like them clothes you got on."

"I didn't choose this life. You can't make me feel bad just because of the clothes I wear."

"What are you to him, his squaw? Does he screw you good?"

236

"That's nasty talk. Our people don't talk that way."

"Well, us Americans do. We like to talk real dirty and drink lots of whiskey. Better get used to it."

"He's my papa now and he's a good man," Dolores said. "He loves his son."

"Why didn't you say so? I'll get a fire goin and send up a smoke signal. We'll have his boy back home lickety-split."

"That's not funny."

The old man shook his head. "Lots of papas love their sons. Don't change a damn thing. Neither does gold—the White Eye can offer em all the money in the world, but nothin's goin to bring his boy back from the Indeh."

Indeh, the name the People had taken up when they knew all was lost. It meant the Dead.

The pair of men who'd exited the roadhouse now stood pissing in the lot. One of them looked back over his shoulder and stared at Dolores in the sedan. He elbowed his buddy and nodded toward her.

They zipped up and started walking over. The clean-shaven one had to help his staggering friend, pulling him aside when he almost stepped in a pothole.

They leaned down to look in Dolores's window. "Hey, pretty darlin," the clean-shaven man said. "Name's Kirby. You want to come out and dance?"

Dolores stared straight ahead, ignoring them.

Kirby's friend tapped the glass. "Hey, how much?" he demanded.

"You be nice, Cecil," Kirby told him, "and she'll be nice to us. I can tell she's a real nice girl. Ain't you, darlin?"

"Go away," she said.

"Well, that wasn't nice at all. I'm liable to let Cecil bust that window out if you ain't goin to treat me right."

"How much?" Cecil asked again.

Dolores was silent.

Cecil stepped to Dasoda-hae's window. "Wake up, Cochise. How much is she?"

"A bottle of whiskey," the old man said, "and you can have her."

"Can't get one, they done kicked us out."

Kirby took a flask from his pocket. He unscrewed the lid and sipped.

"What you got in there?" Dasoda-hae asked.

"Good stuff. Open up the door, I'll give you a snort."

Dolores turned to them, eyes flashing. She pulled a pocketknife from her purse and opened the blade. "I'll cut your belly open and feed your guts to the coyotes."

"What's a matter with her?" Kirby said. "Acts like she got a cactus up her hootch."

Kirby laughed at his joke, turning to his buddy. He didn't see Jubal step out of the roadhouse, a paperbag under his arm, and take in the scene at a glance.

"You hear that, Cecil? She's goin to feed my guts to the coyotes. Well, I'll tell you somethin, I'm goin to tickle her tonsils first."

Jubal came up behind Kirby and slammed his face against the hood of the Ford. His nose crunched against metal. Kirby dropped to the gravel, out like a light, his nose pouring blood.

Cecil looked at Jubal, then down to Kirby. He spat tobacco juice on the unconscious man's forehead.

"He wasn't no friend of mine, mister," Cecil said.

Jubal set the paperbag on the hood and stepped over Kirby.

"I got a condition," Cecil said. "I got me this condition where I bleed real easy and it won't hardly stop."

"Well, if you didn't have it before," Jubal told him, "you're fixin to."

Cecil turned and scurried through the rows of cars, but Jubal followed him deep into the dark lot.

Dolores returned the pocketknife to her purse.

"Roll down your window, girl," Dasoda-hae said. "Reach me that good whiskey."

* * *

When Jubal slid behind the wheel, Dolores saw his shirt was stained with blood. For a moment before firing the ignition he sat rubbing his knuckles. Dolores didn't speak.

"That'll show them palefaces," the old scout said. He raised his bottle in toast.

They drove back toward the reservation. The moon

rose over sand dunes, its cold light silvering the road and the wasteland.

"All right, you've got your damn whiskey," Jubal said.

"Want a sip?" Dasoda-hae asked.

"I want to know if you can get a message to the broncos."

"Pull over up here. I need to stretch my legs."

Jubal didn't slow down. "Can you do it or not?"

"Pull over and we'll talk."

Jubal swore. He braked and turned off the asphalt and parked with the headlights on rolling dunes.

Dasoda-hae opened his door and climbed out. He went around the Ford carrying his whiskey and started walking up a dune.

"Where the hell are you goin?" Jubal asked. He killed the engine. He stepped out with Dolores and they leaned against the hood and watched the old Apache under the bright moon.

He drank and stared across the desert floor. After a while he said, "Goyathlay, the one you White Eyes call Geronimo, he was a troublemaker. His band always raidin and killin, makin life hard for the ones who stayed on the reservation. The White Eyes treated us all the same. Blamed us for everything Geronimo did. He wouldn't stay on the rez and die like a good Indin, like the rest of us. I was young then. I thought if we was honorable and stopped the fightin, the government would do right by us. Give us our freedom. Back then I figured it was the only way to save my people, so I joined the scouts. They gave me a red headband, showed me how to march and salute."

He straightened his back and stood at attention, tossed them his best salute. He took a pull from the bottle. "The army trained me not to think, just do whatever the son of a bitch Al Sieber told me to. I led Crook through the sierras and hunted the Chiricahua with that one-eyed coyote Mickey Free. I hunted em on account of the government promised not to kill us all and the Chiricahuas ain't my band anyway."

"Does this story have a point to it?" Jubal asked.

"I paid for everything I ever done to my people. The government sent my boy to a school in Pennsylvania. His momma and me didn't hear nothin for a year. Then a letter comes one day, says our boy got sick with consumption and died. My wife stabbed herself in the heart that summer and now I got my boy's sickness."

He came slowly down the dune and stood facing Jubal. "I wish every government in the world was sunk a mile deep in White Eye hell and I was burnin right there with em. What do you think of that?"

"I think you talk too much for an Indian."

"Who are you callin Indin? I'm a damn all-American." He chuckled and coughed. Finally he said, "You want to know about the sierras."

"If you can get a message through, I'll give you a

thousand dollars and all the whiskey you can drink."

"You know why Geronimo surrendered? He thought maybe the government would let him and his people live like human beings. But the soldiers herded em onto a train instead and sent em to a bad place called Florida. Without the scouts, the army would've been fightin for another thirty years, but did they get any thanks? Not even mercy. The scouts that was Chiricahua, they got put on the train too and they all went to die together."

He jabbed his finger in Jubal's chest. "Your word's no good. Not to the Indeh, the ones in the sierras. They didn't lay down their guns with Geronimo. They know when a White Eye promises life, he means death and plenty of it. Go home and try to forget you ever had a son."

Jubal rubbed his aching knuckles.

Dolores stepped up to the old man. She reached and took his hand. Dasoda-hae looked startled at her touch. As though it had been many years since another reached out to him. He didn't pull away.

"Please, Grandfather," Dolores said. "Help us."

"It won't do no good talkin to em."

"Please," she said.

He stared at the girl a long time, silent. Then he said, "All right, Granddaughter. The Indeh will hear your message. I promise it."

"Any price," Jubal said. "I want them to know I'll give anything for John Russell."

Dasoda-hae turned to him. "There ain't no money can buy back the dead. The girl knows. Maybe she don't have the heart to tell you, but she knows the truth."

* * *

In Douglas on their return Jubal took her to a picture show, a matinée before the train back across the border, the first movie she'd ever seen. Dolores sat in the dim theatre, her eyes fixed on galloping horses and cowboys fanning six-shooters, Indian marauders with great feathered headdresses. Her popcorn forgotten, going untouched. Though the movie was filled with inaccuracies, careless and comic mistakes, there were also surely a few stray images that had been part of her old life. Yet the idea of a parallel between reality and what she saw on the screen never occurred to the girl. She didn't imagine herself as a character in the story. She accepted it as offered and she wasn't disappointed. In the end the villainous chief lay dead and the cowboy leaned from his white horse to sweep up his beloved in his arms and they rode into the setting sun.

When they stepped outside into the bright desert light, Jubal asked what she'd thought. The Apache girl stood in her cloche hat and high heels and said she liked it. She wouldn't mind seeing it again sometime.

CHAPTER ELEVEN

On a spring morning the village gathered to witness the boy receive his new name. At sunrise he kneeled in silence while Nantan sang a prayer over him.

The boy had won the People's acceptance defeating Coyote. They saw him as their own. No longer did he perform chores for the women, but spent his days playing and training with the other youths. Even his little brothers held him in newfound respect after the way he'd dispatched his opponent.

On his knees he stared up at the medicine man. Nantan streaked the boy's brow with hoddentin, the sacred pollen of the tule, and finished his song.

Carnoviste stepped forward and stood over the boy.

"Denali, my son," he said. "Let this be your name all your life."

Carnoviste held out his hand, a shard of charcoal on his palm. The boy recalled his instructions, what he must do next, and he took the charcoal and spat on it and threw it to the east.

"That was my old name," he recited. "I don't want it

anymore. Let me be called by my true name all my life."

From that time on, he was Denali.

* * *

Around the fire Denali listened close when Nantan spoke of the People's past, their distant origins.

"We walked down from a cold country in the north," he said. "Long ago, before the White Eyes came. The grandfathers used to speak of it. A place of ice and wind. Some of the young don't believe it—nobody knows where we came from, they say. These braves are like a man who falls asleep under a great tree and sleeps so long the tree withers and dies and is cut for firewood. Then the sleeper wakes and doesn't know where he is or which way to go forward anymore. The fool—all he had to do was dig in the earth to find the roots still there. Those who forget the past are lost and wander as the cursed."

Then he would tell the old stories. Children listened rapt to tales of the People's legendary heroes, Killer of Enemies, White Painted Woman, and Child of the Waters who slew the monster called Yeh Yeh. When he finished one tale, they'd beg for another, nothing they loved to hear more.

* * *

The People's tongue became the language of his dreams. It was only then he saw wonders he couldn't explain.

Denali saw the medicine man one evening dance about the fire and take a knife from his moccasin. He saw Nantan turn the blade on himself and plunge it into his own breast and how the blood did flow. Then Gouyen passed her brother a burning cigarette. He smoked and the smoke appeared from the wound in his chest, the blood and smoke together, and the medicine man danced on.

Another occasion after days of fasting Nantan called them, old and young, to form a circle around him while he stood motionless and sang. The crowd echoed his song. After a while they witnessed first his heels, then his toes begin rising from the ground. He levitated above the village, slowly ascending until Denali shielded his eyes against the sun to look where he hovered in the sky.

"Such Power," Ishton whispered.

The look on Carnoviste's face was grim, troubled.

"What mortal hand has Power to slay me?" Nantan spoke from the air. "Who can come against the People? My Power is strong enough to swallow up our enemies like a hungry bear and no warrior can slay me."

In that moment Denali felt himself purged of doubt. The medicine man could never be killed, he knew it, and the People had no reason to fear. Even in the darkest times his Power would preserve them.

"I don't understand," Denali said later. "Why didn't I

see these miracles before? Why didn't I see them when I first came to live with the People?"

"What are you talking about, my son?" Carnoviste said. "Of course you saw such things. Did you forget all the times we watched Nantan show off his Power? What silliness. You know better."

* * *

His hair grew long. One night he held those red locks back from his face and stood like a perfect servant while Ishton took an awl of carved bone, its tip sharpened to a fine point, and pierced his earlobe. Afterward the earring he wore was a small blue stone.

Constant practice made him quick and accurate with the bow. In target games among friends the object was to land his arrow closest against his opponent's. Losers surrendered their finely crafted arrows to the victor and soon Denali amassed a large collection.

For long stretches each day he trained with his companions under Carnoviste's watchful eye. They'd line up and take a mouthful of water before heading out in a slow run across the plateau. When they reached the cliff edge, they turned and ran back, still holding the water in their mouths. It forced them to learn proper breathing in the thin mountain air, how to set a pace they could maintain for great distances.

"Don't spring with your full measure," Carnoviste

said. "Not till you're coming up on the finish. Keep a reserve."

This was the most arduous of all their practice. No one despised it more than Denali, but he knew better than to complain.

"Obedience is survival," Carnoviste told them. He stood with his switch in hand. "Don't count on Power alone to keep you alive. You need a strong will and it's my place to teach you strength."

Denali's skin was pale beside the dark boys, but they called him brother and he made friends with a novice warrior his own age. Chatto, the son of Zunde. Chatto had already accompanied his father on a brief raid, acting as the warriors' orderly and seeing to their mounts. Like all novices he'd remained confined to camp work. Only after four raids were behind him could he participate in the plunder.

Chatto told wild tales of things he claimed to have seen on the raid, presumably while holding the horses or fixing meals. These exaggerated exploits were a source of great pride to him and jealousy to the other boys, all save Denali.

The prospect of raiding held little appeal to Denali. He preferred wandering the woods alone with his bow, letting his thoughts run free. Chatto ragged him for keeping to himself. Even the warriors grew concerned at the time the boy spent alone—it wasn't like the People to be so solitary and it spoke of a warped nature. Denali overheard them talking with Carnoviste, the warriors arguing it was time for him to learn the path of raiding. Every brave was needed when they came of age.

Carnoviste defended him. "It's not important he should mature as soon as an apple tree or an oak. Denali is my son. He'll learn what it means to be a warrior when I say he's ready."

* * *

A group of wives and maidens were preparing to gather wildberries in the woods above the village. The work of picking berries wasn't without danger. Bears loved the taste of the sweet fruit and encounters with them could turn deadly.

Carnoviste called Denali and Chatto to his side. "Go with the women and guard them. Keep your eyes and ears open. Don't let yourself be distracted with childish things, understand me?"

"Yes, my chief," the boys spoke in unison.

"Wait here," Carnoviste said. He ducked into his wickiup.

"You know what this means?" Chatto asked.

"It's a warrior's job," Denali said.

"If he trusts you to guard the women, you're ready to join us on the next raid. I look forward to riding with you, my brother."

Denali looked troubled.

Carnoviste emerged gripping a rifle, a battered Trapdoor Springfield, and handed it to Chatto along with a pouch of old .45-70 blackpowder cartridges. "You'll carry the rifle," Carnoviste said, "because you've proven yourself on a raid. Let me see you load it."

The weapon took its name from the hinged breechblock that opened like a trapdoor. The hammer had a three-click tumbler. Its first notch was safety or half-cock, the second was the loading position, allowing the trapdoor to open, and third was ready to fire.

Chatto took a cartridge from the pouch. He pulled the hammer back two clicks and flipped open the breechblock and inserted the cartridge and snapped the trapdoor shut. When he eased the hammer down to half-cock, Carnoviste nodded his approval.

"Good," the chief said. He turned to Denali. "My son, take your bow and quiver."

"Yes, my chief."

"Work together and don't forget your duty."

Chatto's grin stretched wide. "Let's go."

Denali retrieved his bow and arrows, then they departed with the women. Chatto took the lead, the rifle yoked across his shoulders, and they crossed the grassland to the foot of the pine-topped ridge. Heading up the crooked trail Chatto walked point while Denali followed behind the group with his bow in hand. Ishton lingered in the rear, hanging back beside him.

"Only a trusted young brave may guard the women,"

she said. "Your father believes in your skill and judgement."

It was in Denali to feel pride at being chosen for the task, but thinking of Carnoviste as his father was strange, impossible to accept. He couldn't forget all that had occurred when they'd taken him and left his White Eye family dead in the valley, but in the boy's mind Carnoviste was his chief.

"He gave Chatto the rifle," Denali said.

"Because he's ridden with the warriors," Ishton told him. "Next time we gather berries, you'll have a rifle too."

"I don't know if I want to go raiding."

"You won't always feel that way. It's part of the warrior's life. Someday you'll be proud to join them."

"Maybe," he said, still unsure.

Ishton smiled. "I know you will."

She wore her hair in a long braid tucked into her belt to avoid catching it among the brambles they'd be working in. A woven basket rested in the crook of her arm. The skirt of her buckskin dress was short and her moccasins rose to her knees.

Denali thought she was very beautiful. They walked in the cool shadows of the pines and when she smiled back at him over her shoulder, something in him ached with a pain he'd never known until now. He had to remind himself to keep his eyes on the woods—he'd been charged with a serious responsibility, one he couldn't betray.

When they reached the thicket where the wildberries grew, Gouyen was the first into the brush. She went without hesitation, without pause. Unlike her to be so rash. The other women stopped to sing a medicine song and shake the branches, causing a racket to alert wild four-legs of their presence.

Gouyen reached out to pluck a fruit. A slight tremor in her hand. Denali noticed her face was pallid and she appeared weak from the long hike, impatient to taste of the refreshing berries. She tugged the berry free and brought it to her mouth and ate.

The women entered the brush and started picking.

The wildberries had only just begun to ripen. Perhaps they'd been hasty, too eager for sweetness after winter's austerity, because now they were forced to move deep into the thicket to find enough of the ripe fruit. Creeping vines wove a tangled carpet and made walking difficult. Chatto and Denali kept the group between them, joining the women in the brambles.

Something in the air.

Denali sniffed.

A faint tinge, vaguely familiar. He couldn't say what it was or why he felt sudden disquiet.

The women filled their baskets. After a while Denali became aware they were slowly breaking into two groups, those closest to Chatto drifting east, following Gouyen as she moved to the far edge of the thicket.

Too much distance was increasing between the point and rear guard.

He was poised to call out, ready to tell them to move back together, when Ishton stepped toward him. She held out a berry on her palm. "They're so good. Try one."

He reached for her hand, then froze.

"What's wrong?" she asked.

"Can you smell that?"

The odor had strengthened with their progress into the thicket. At first he'd thought it was a rabbit dead in the undergrowth, but this was too strong, a strange reeking, heavy in the air.

Then he recognized it. Fear wrapped itself around his spinal column and he stood straight and rigid.

He grabbed Ishton's hand, crushing the berry. Like blood between their palms.

"Run," he yelled. "It's a bear! Everybody run."

Even as he shouted the warning it rose up from the brush, the grizzly standing on its hindlegs, enormous and so close Denali couldn't believe his eyes. As though it had been lying in wait.

The bear towered over them. Its fur was a dark brown, almost black. A shape like a white star on its chest. The Power of the women's song should have frightened it off—this was unusual behavior, even from a grizzly.

The women ran. They dropped their baskets and crashed through the twisted vines and thorns, all save

Gouyen, who stood rooted, staring at the pale star as though transfixed.

The grizzly lunged and snatched up a running woman. It was Alopay, the plump young wife of Jolsanny, and she screamed in the beast's embrace.

Denali let go of Ishton's hand. He rushed at the bear and reached behind his back to the quiver, drawing an arrow. He nocked it and pulled the string taut and set the arrow flying.

The tip buried in the grizzly's chest, impaling the white star.

Gouyen turned and ran.

The bear roared, then its jaws clamped down on Alopay's arm. The grizzly wrenched its head from side to side and tore the girl's arm from her body. The severed appendage fell in the brush.

Blood jetted. Alopay's eyes flickered and she went limp.

Denali loosed a quick succession of arrows and they pierced the bear's flesh in a cluster of feathered shafts. Blood ran from the wounds, but otherwise all his efforts were in vain. The bear appeared not even to notice. Denali shouted and waved his arms, hoping to cower it, make it release the girl, and in his mind he was begging Chatto to hurry with the rifle.

* * *

Chatto ran staggering through the vines. How could so much distance have spread between them? He cursed himself for not noticing the gap separating the groups of berry pickers.

When he rushed out from behind a stand of trees, he saw the bear ahead, a giant grizzly with Alopay in its clutches. Chatto brought the rifle to his shoulder and pulled back the hammer. Just as he pulled the trigger, a pair of fleeing maidens dashed across his line of fire. In the split second before the rifle fired he moved the barrel a fraction.

Life and death in a hair's breadth—

The bullet missed the maidens and the bear.

* * *

A rifleshot cracked. Denali saw Chatto with the Springfield against his shoulder, a great plume of smoke issuing from the barrel.

The bear dropped Alopay to the ground. At first Denali thought Chatto's shot had stunned the bear. Then it lowered itself and placed a huge forepaw on Alopay's chest and took the girl's head between its teeth.

Denali cried out and pulled his knife from his moccasin. He made a mad charge toward the beast.

* * *

Chatto's movements were automatic, his hands a blur of motion. Yet it seemed to him as if he struggled through a thick aether that slowed the world to a crawl while his mind raged faster than light. He pulled the Springfield's hammer back two notches and opened the trapdoor. The extractor kicked out the empty shell, smoke rising from the breechblock, and he fumbled with a cartridge from the pouch, got it in, and flipped down the trapdoor and pulled the hammer back all the way. He raised the barrel once more.

* * *

There was an awful crunch and Denali drew up and stared at Alopay in the wildberry bushes, her skull crushed.

Chatto fired again.

The bear shuddered when it took a fleshwound in the side. It growled and lumbered a few feet before dropping down out of sight, there one instant, vanished the next.

Chatto reloaded. Denali stood watching the undergrowth, waiting, the air heavy with the mingled smell of blackpowder and the stench of the beast.

"Where did it go?" Chatto asked when he had another cartridge chambered.

Denali shook his head. The grizzly was too big, even on all fours, to be entirely concealed by the brush. Then he caught movement. The vegetation shaking, limbs trembling at its passage, and he realized there was a hidden wash running through the thicket. It was a narrow gully cut by rainwater off the slope and the bear was escaping down its length.

"It's in a gully," Denali yelled.

Chatto followed the shaking brush with his rifle barrel. He hesitated, wanting to fire into the brush but knowing how long it took to reload the rifle, too long for a wasted round—he had to wait till he had a clear shot.

The grizzly bounded out of the gully. It charged into the trees, moving faster than Denali would've believed possible for a creature its size and Chatto's final shot slammed into a pine trunk, then the killer was out of sight in the deep woods.

Denali kneeled beside Alopay. He turned her body over and looked at her face and forever afterward wished he hadn't.

His hands shook in rage at what the grizzly had done, rage at the thought of how easily it could've been Ishton dead on the ground.

* * *

Most of the women had run back down the trail. Denali and Chatto gathered the few who remained on the ridgeside and started out for the village. They were reluctant to leave Alopay's body, but she was a big woman. It would take both of the boys to carry her and they refused to let their weapons leave their hands.

They descended to the pasture and crossed at a run.

In the village the warriors were already taking up rifles. A number of women had arrived breathless and terrified with news of the attack. Now Carnoviste saw the last of the berry pickers coming and he strained to see who was absent. He spotted Ishton, then Denali. The relief on his face was impossible to conceal.

"Who's missing?" he shouted.

"The wife of Jolsanny," Denali said. Even in the panic he observed the custom of refraining from speaking the name of the dead.

At this Jolsanny let out a cry of grief and fury. He started toward the wooded slope, but Carnoviste grabbed his arm.

"Wait," he said. "We need Nantan, or we'll never get close enough to kill it."

Only a medicine man with Bear Power could hunt a grizzly successfully and without risk of the bear sickness. Unless Nantan joined their party they had little hope of finding the killer.

"His wickiup is empty," Zunde said.

"He's gone looking for herbs on the ridge," Gouyen told them. It was the first she'd spoken since the attack and she was still breathing hard from the run. "Maybe he'll find you in the woods."

Carnoviste got out his 1903 Springfield, the bolt-action rifle with its five-round clip much improved over Chatto's single-shot breechloader. He tied an ammo pouch to his belt. Then he chose five men for the hunting party, including Jolsanny and Zunde. He asked two older warriors to join them as far as the thicket and carry down Alopay's body.

They set out. Denali grabbed a fresh quiver of arrows and ran after them.

Carnoviste glanced over his shoulder. "You have to stay, my son."

"My arrows are in the bear's chest. I need to finish it."

"Go back. Hunting bears is for warriors—you're not ready."

"I saw what it did to her. I saw her face. Let me go with you—I have to do this."

Carnoviste slowed and looked at him. "All right," he said. "You can come." He pulled a revolver from his belt and handed it to the boy. Denali ran beside the men, gripping his new pistol.

Now Chatto caught them up. "Father, can I go too?"

Zunde frowned and started to shake his head.

"Is my friend more of a warrior than I am?" Chatto asked.

"Fine," Zunde told him. "Don't slow us down."

The boys ran on with the warriors.

* * *

Jolsanny fell to his knees when he saw her. His wife had suffered a fate worse than mere death. Now she must go through eternity in the Other World with her face disfigured and her arm missing.

The widowed man gripped his knife and slashed his hair. He drew the blade across his palm and let the red droplets fall and stain the leaves.

They crossed the thicket and the hidden wash. Carnoviste found the tracks and blood, the same tracks as the time before at the hollow tree, a bear with a twisted left hindpaw. Its trail ran up the hillside, blood on the undergrowth every few steps.

"Should we wait until Nantan comes back?" Pericho asked.

"There's no time," Carnoviste said. "We can't risk letting it get away. This bear has a bad hunger."

Moh-tsos and Jlin-Litzoque stayed behind to carry the body back to the village. For a moment Denali was afraid Carnoviste would change his mind and task Chatto and himself with that duty, but the chief feared leaving the boys alone while the grizzly remained on the loose.

They followed the tracks. Carnoviste led them along a winding game trail through the pines. At first everything was as it should've been, but after a while a strange realization struck Denali—the blood had stopped.

"Where's the blood?" he asked. "It was all over the ground before, now it's gone."

"You're right," Chatto said. "Why did it stop?"

"He should still be bleeding. He's carrying too many of my arrows and you shot him once. We should still see blood."

None of the warriors offered comment, but Denali could see it disturbed them as well.

The tracks went up a steep ascent and their climb slowed as the ground turned to naked stone. They struggled to the top of a bluff and stood on a rough dome of fissured rock, flat and barren, where nothing could leave any sign of passage. The bones of deer and sheep and mountain lions lay scattered.

Nantan sat alone, waiting for them.

They paused in surprise, startled to see the medicine man in that lonesome place. A feeling of unease came over Denali, the same dread he'd experienced in the thicket, the dread in the hollow tree. He tightened his hold on the pistol.

"How did you find us here?" Zunde asked.

Nantan didn't answer. He gripped his staff, carved with stars and halfmoons and other glyphs more curious yet. He wore a breechclout and he was bare-chested. He rose slowly to his feet, unarmed, and came limping toward them, the tip of his staff knocking on stone, bear claws dancing around his neck.

Denali took in his crippled gait, the tattoo of a black star on his chest. He glanced at Chatto and their eyes held a moment, the selfsame unspeakable thought passing between them.

"Where were you?" Jolsanny asked. "We needed your Bear Power."

"I was gathering herbs," Nantan said, "when I sensed something was wrong. My Power led me here and I waited for you to come."

"A grizzly attacked the women," Carnoviste told him.

"Was anyone hurt?"

"Jolsanny's wife is dead. We tracked the grizzly up here."

Bones everywhere. All bore teethmarks and a number of them lay in odd little piles. As though cast in divination.

"What is this place?" Zunde wondered. "The bear must be witched."

Denali turned and looked out from that high dome. The sun was sinking and a honeycolored light suffused the woods below. He could see beyond the pasture to where the village lay small in the distance and he wondered if the predator often watched their lives from above.

"Don't worry," Nantan told them. "Even if it's witched, it can't harm you while you're with me."

"The bear ripped my wife apart," Jolsanny whispered. "It's evil."

The medicine man shook his head. "Were there no guards protecting the women?"

"These boys did all they could," Carnoviste said.

Nantan limped to Denali and Chatto. He placed his hands on their shoulders. "Don't blame yourselves, boys. Only one with Bear Power can defeat this monster. You're lucky it didn't kill you as well."

They nodded, careful not to meet his eyes.

In the waning light Carnoviste and Zunde circled the overlook, cutting for sign in the vegetation along its rim. They found nothing. There was a single route the bear could've taken downward without leaving a clear trail. At one edge of the dome a precipitous slope, in places near vertical, led through a jumble of broken rocks.

"You think it went that way?" Zunde asked.

Carnoviste hesitated. It was difficult to accept such a large bear could've negotiated the slope, but what other explanation?

"It's the only way it could've gone," he said.

Zunde stared. "Then this bear is definitely witched."

"We should check down below for tracks. We'll have to go back the way we came, then circle around."

"The sun's almost gone. It would be too dark to see by the time we got down there."

Nothing more could be done.

"From now on," Carnoviste said, "four warriors will guard the women when they go out. This can't happen again."

Zunde turned to the medicine man. "We're witched from following this bear. Will you sing protection over us?"

"Kneel down and I'll perform the cleansing."

The hunting party kneeled upon the rock. Nantan started singing, dancing a circle around them, and he opened a pouch and poured sacred pollen onto his palm and sprinkled each of them.

Chatto leaned close to Denali's ear. "The star, his leg…" he whispered.

Denali nodded.

Just like the bear.

* * *

On the return Denali and Chatto were silent, the horror still fresh in their minds, wishing they'd been more alert and heeded their impressions of danger before the bear struck. Alopay's crushed face haunted Denali as though its image were burned upon his eyes. He wondered if the guilt would ever leave him.

In the village he surrendered the pistol to Carnoviste. Then Ishton came and hugged him and he fought back sudden tears.

Later that evening with the howls of Jolsanny's grief rising from the dark, the boys walked off alone. The question hung over them. At last Chatto gave it voice.

"Could it be true?" he asked.

"I keep thinking of when I ran away and hid in the woods," Denali said.

"And the bear almost got you."

"Nantan was in the woods that day too. We met him coming back."

"This is bad," Chatto said.

"What can we do?"

"We can't tell anyone."

Denali knew he was right. The medicine man was too highly-regarded. Even more than the People's trust, he had their love. Who would believe such a thing? Especially when his accusers were a pair of boys who'd failed in their duty to guard the women. All they had was suspicion and coincidence. They'd need proof—for themselves as much as anyone.

"But could Nantan be so powerful?" Denali wondered. "To turn himself into a bear?" His mind railed against the absurdity. Then he thought of all the miracles he'd witnessed the medicine man perform.

"How else can you explain it?" Chatto asked.

"But my arrows and your bullet, we both hit the bear. When we met Nantan, he wasn't hurt."

"You've seen him stab his heart with the knife. You've seen the blood, then later there's never a mark."

"Why wasn't he stuck with my arrows still?"

"Maybe he pulled your arrows out and threw them so far in the brush that we missed them. His Power heals him fast, that's why the blood went away on the trail."

"It can't be true," Denali said.

"What would convince you?"

"I'd have to watch him changing, becoming the bear."

A cry from Jolsanny's ragged throat cut through the night. The boys shuddered at the sound.

"I can't stop seeing her face," Denali confessed.

"Me neither."

There was a silence. Then Denali said, "We need proof. We have to know for sure before we tell Carnoviste."

"When Nantan goes out alone, we'll follow him."

"If we're right and he finds us on his trail, he'll kill us both."

"There's no choice," Chatto said. "Nobody else suspects it. I'd rather die than watch more of our People get killed."

Denali nodded. "We have to stop the bear."

TO BE CONTINUED…

**The story picks up in *Deathsong*, book two of the Beloved Captive Trilogy …
Can Denali and Chatto discover proof of the medicine man's secret?**

Read the first chapter of *Deathsong* and get your copy now!

DEATHSONG

MAX McNABB

BELOVED CAPTIVE TRILOGY BOOK 2

DEATHSONG
MAX McNABB

Beloved Captive Trilogy Book 2

The Power of their song failed to protect the women from the beast. It had risen from hiding and fallen among the wives and maidens in the woods where they were picking wildberries. Ravenous, tearing. Now Alopay must enter the Other World missing an arm. The boys assigned to watch over the berry-pickers had struck back, but Denali's arrows and Chatto's Springfield rifle weren't enough to kill the grizzly.

Nights following the attack Denali would jolt awake in his wickiup, images haunting all his dreams. Alopay's crushed skull, her lifeless eyes. The white shape like a star on the grizzly's chest, slowly blackening until it was the dark star tattooed above Nantan's heart. The medicine man had a crooked left foot—the grizzly's left hindpaw was twisted inward. Such coincidence was a curious thing.

After the bear escaped down a gully hidden in the undergrowth, Denali and Chatto joined the hunting party. The blood trail soon dried up, but the warriors happened upon the beast's feeding place, a rock dome overlooking the village below, and there sat Nantan as though awaiting them. The medicine man explained he'd been searching for herbs on the ridgeside when his Power told him something was wrong and led him to that place of bones.

"If the bear is witched," Nantan told them, "only my Power can defeat it."

The warriors felt great comfort to have their trusted medicine man at their side, but Chatto and Denali shared a look between them. The star on Nantan's chest, the crooked left foot—could such a thing be?

They spoke only to each other of their dark suspicion. No one else could know. The People loved their medicine man too well. Nantan was an immortal, it was said—and not without reason to believe it. Denali himself had seen Nantan cut his own chest with a blade, deep and bloody, and he'd seen the wounded flesh quickening, closing. The only wounds he couldn't fully heal were those he'd suffered long ago as a young man when a grizzly lamed his foot and scarred his face. Nantan's Power was great and no one could deny it, but had that Power turned to the witching way? Had the medicine man transformed himself into the beast?

They had to be sure before they told the chief of their

suspicions.

Over the following days Denali and Chatto kept a close watch. Nantan stayed in the camp, curtailing for a time his usual practice of wandering alone, but Denali and Chatto remained vigilant. Often it seemed half a game with them, the boys playing warriors on a secret mission, then the face of Alopay would rise up and they'd remember their duty for the grave enterprise it was.

After a few days the women were ready for a return to the thicket. They gathered berries without incident, Carnoviste and three other warriors standing by, and there was no further sign of the grizzly.

At last came the morning when Nantan took up his staff and limped out of the village. Denali and Chatto watched him crossing the pasture, heading for the rise of pines, and they gave him a long lead, allowing him to enter the woods before they set out armed with bows and full quivers.

Denali believed himself a decent tracker, but Chatto was a master. They trailed the medicine man up the slope and past the berry thicket. Denali watched his friend's eyes scanning the ground and undergrowth, noting the impression of Nantan's staff, spiderwebs ripped at his passing, and then the ground was rocky, torn lichen alone pointing them on.

They walked side by side. They walked like Child of the Waters and Killer of Enemies together in an older time, gone out to slay the monster.

For a while it appeared the trail was taking them to the overlook, the place of bones. Fear fluttered like a raven in their bellies. There was no way to approach the high bluff without being observed from above. Then Nantan's course swung away, moving instead toward a secluded meadow Denali once visited on his own wanderings, and they followed him through the trees, silent and intent.

They were no more than a stride from the trunk of a great pine when Gouyen stepped out from behind it. She stood before them gripping a long knife.

The boys were as shocked as though the grizzly itself had leapt upon them.

"Where are you little rabbits going?" she demanded.

She stared through cold eyes like the eyes of the dead and her knife dangled from a gnarled hand. In his mind Denali saw the blade dripping with his mother's blood.

They were speechless.

"Why are you following my brother?" she asked. "Don't you know there's a bear in these woods who loves to eat up little rabbits?"

It was Denali who recovered first. "That's why we're following Nantan. To protect him from the bear. It's not safe for him to wander alone."

"The People couldn't survive without our medicine man," Chatto spoke up. "He needs warriors to guard him."

"And you think you're the warriors for the job," Gouyen said.

Chatto stood straight. "I'd die for the People."

She slipped the knife into its sheath under the fold of her moccasin. "Nantan is immortal. Have you forgotten my brother's Power? No two-legs or four-legs can harm him. He doesn't need you to protect him from the bear or anything else. You understand?"

They nodded.

"Now go back," she said. "Hunt something for the stewpot like good boys. You'll have time enough to be warriors later."

They turned to go. Denali hesitated, then looked back.

"Did you hear us coming?" he asked. "If we're to be warriors, we can't make that kind of mistake again."

"I followed you following Nantan," she told him. "I was behind you the whole way until the end when I ran ahead. It was you who didn't hear me coming."

Denali nodded and started back down with Chatto. They shared a look, thinking the same thought once more—it was impossible. Even if they hadn't sensed her on their backtrail, they'd have heard her moving through the undergrowth to advance on them. Gouyen hadn't followed them.

She'd been waiting in the woods.

Waiting for Nantan.

Get your copy of *Deathsong* to continue the epic story!

Made in the USA
Coppell, TX
06 October 2022